IS

IS

FORM & OTHER FORMS

Martin Nakell

ISBN: 978-1-943170-04-3

Cover Design: Jane L. Carman
Interior Design: Paige Domantey
Production Director: Jane L. Carman

Typeface: Baskerville

Published by: Lit Fest Press, Carman, 688 Knox Road 900 North, Gilson, Illinois 61436

festivalwriter.org

TABLE OF CONTENTS

ONE

in midnight darkness the ballpark shimmers when the old volcano erupts the people escape on the backs of stampeding elephants i can attest to the existence of alternate universes i have been there so have you but you may not remember in a bullet filled world we zigzag our way back to midnight when i call you on the telephone i answer my voice bounces off the moon when you answer the one thing that's assured is relief and redemption is the opening of the gates of paradise to the mundanity[1] of everywhere of is won't you come back charlie parker to invent us again won't you serenade the barefoot girl who sees only beauty in all of the senses who embraces the coming and going of ideas made into water and what about the other one who softened the edges of time using irrational numbers and what about the one we read about in the newspapers who walked on water but couldn't swim through the midnight air and then

---

1   "Anglo-Norman mundain, mundan, mundein, mondan and Middle French, French mondain worldly, earthly (late 12th cent. in Anglo-Norman as mundain , also 14th cent. in a Picard text in this form; c1225 in Old French in sense 'secular', c1275 in sense 'cosmic', c1480 as noun in sense 'person fond of worldly pleasures', 1498 denoting a dweller in the earthly world in the passage translated in quot. 1509 at sense B. 1; compare mondaine adj., mondain n., mondaine n.) and their etymon classical Latin mundānus belonging to the world, earthly, relating to the universe, cosmic (earliest attested 2nd cent. a.d. in Apuleius, but compare earlier use as noun), in post-classical Latin also secular (4th cent.) and in astrological sense (c1230 in a British source), also in classical Latin as noun in sense 'inhabitant of the world' (Cicero, translating ancient Greek κοσμοπολίτης cosmopolite n.), in post-classical Latin also secular person (4th cent.) < mundus world (of uncertain origin) + -ānus -ane suffix" (Oxford English Dictionary. Online Edition. 13 December 2014).

comes the world-round holiday when everyone fasting by feasting on locally grown foods watches the president of the world on television pantomime laughing weeping screaming a serious face a look of wonder shock and awe she removes her clown suit to reveal that she is the archangel gabriel who in the hindu tradition is the diety of patience and compassion and who in the cultural tradition of the south pacific islanders is a mythical figure throwing flames into the sea and in certain parts of africa is the sun god whose heat stretches tight the drumheads as the drums come alive while in the great levant it is the olive tree which is not an object of worship but a testimony of the eternal return ripeness and all for these things we give thanks and for that which brought us here where we never thought to be never even dreamed to arrive never believed in and will never forget we who are so human it's unbelievable to know ourselves

for Rebbeca Len Ravi

AN ERASURE

1.
everything is erased

2.
the city under the bridge
is where the police
chase only the police
is where the distance of any journey
is twice as long in returning as in going
but takes only half the time
because of the relationship
of time to topography
which is neither verse nor inverse
to the civic notion
of order
nor to the city's intuitive notion
of disorder
but to the physics
of the eternal return
to the return
to the eternal city
is where each votercitizen
receiving a ballot with but one candidate: freedom
must choose

is where each artist must be
her or his own revolution or be banned

from the Union of It Made New
to be enacted by the Committee
for the Committee to Annihilate Stale
Obvious Egregious Easy Sleazy Boring
& Cheap Sentimentality

is where traffic laws are ignored
because the cars are all invisible because
motion remains a mystery of the quantum experience
of now & is & will & will be

is where the benches arranged
along the rivershore
beneath the bridge
fill with citizens
waiting to be born
urgent
with the desire
for birth pregnant
with the mind
of birth
they will not take no
for an answer they will not
hear yes
but once
over and over again
on the rivershore

is where the suspension
of currency leads to the genesis
of a superfluity of synapses
that join the network criss / crossing
the mind
of the city

3.

the city beneath the bridge has no boundaries
and the name of the city is a name without end
or it is the City Without End

whoever ever enters
the City Without End
becomes a Citizen-
Without-Number

at the citycore
a radiant orb
of a discernible material
spreads to the noborders
it could be anything
but it is inexorable

at the citycore
a controlled backfire
burns the text we write
the uncontrollable poems
on the seedfeeding ashes

at the citycore
the whitest building on earth
rises over the horizon
cutting the edge of tradition
into speculae
businessmen discuss
their affairs in the streets
they dissect
the triangle encircled by the circle
into its component parts
to reenact new forms
of trade i.e. how many
bushels of air for a cow

how many musical notes
would trade
for the fragrance of energy
as embodied in the leaf of the basil
or the stem of labor
in the cityparks the mothers
and the fathers worry
about the safety of their children
if a coming war
between the east & west winds
where to shelter
potential where
to harness the day
of the shadows how
to discover
the beginning of time
how to release it into the framework
of thought

FORMICIDAE [HYMENOPTERA]

for Suzanne Goodman

Ants tunnel pathways which reiterate systems: spiders' webs, cerebral neurons, ganglia, ancient or contemporary earth- or air- or sea-bound pathways, the disruptions then reroutings of a novel, a dialogue no matter what the presumptive subject, a hand with its five fingers, many old and modern paintings, the exponential branching of friendships or families. Is it coincidental that we occupy a world that includes ants, as well as a world that is not an image of itself or a metaphor for anything?

As a rural child he would watch ants. No matter what his mood or psyche he would never harm them. Sometimes with a thin branch he would divert their path to see what they would do to reveal their intelligence. He never thought he was experimenting with nature or watching the stars in the ants or tracing the genealogy of a species. He never thought he was meditating or losing himself or freeing his mind for its limitless or harmless or frightening wanderings. He never thought the way he inverted "ants" to stna and would say to himself stna stna meant anything about language or meaning or gift. He never thought his thought would ever become a problem. He never felt that his thought and his feelings were interrelated or separated. He never thought about what ants thought. He might have assumed they thought/felt what he thought/felt.

An ant with its head cocked to one side :: on the ground, in the grass, a signifier and a signified.

If we experience life as one-hundred percent presence and one-hundred percent absence simultaneously can we study the behavior of the ant to learn anything about biology, physics, phenomenology, astrology, mathematics, music?

it's at apex. a rational world convenes.

Nothing has ever shaken the political stability of ant culture. The political stability of the ant culture has never been shaken, even when ants enslave other ants.

Through hayfields, on ancient paths that stretch around the world, ants toss from attenae to attenae the verb tenses of all languages.

Etymologists in an Australian laboratory have worked to enucleate the ritual conduct of ants, that activity with no functional consequence. They have categorized nine types of ritual to look for in all ant species: (1) formational arrangement of ants which leads to no survival benefit; (2) so-called dream activity or other brain wave anomaly; (3) any behavior by more than one ant at a time which falls outside the parameters of reason; (4) sacrificial murder of an ant of the same nest; (5) the movement in unison by more than one ant at a time of body parts without the movement of bodies; (6) the organized observation of another species; (7) communal attention paid to any object not immediately functional; (8) a response to any change: season, location, diet, age, which yields no adaptive benefit; (9) the appearance of any emotive sign precedent or subsequent to any of the above.

Unnoticed an ant walks on the sidewalk in front of a doorman in front of his building.

Boundaries abound. Abounding, a boundaries. Abetting abut. The line between ant. The distinctions. The line down the middle of the ant, back, then front. The line from the pupil of the right eye to the pupil of the left eye. The boundary of one colony, the boundary of another, the boundary of another. The roaming between boundary and line. The line of the external parameter of the ant, frontal, left, dorsal, right. The line between the art of the ant and the ant. The boundary of the leg. The boundary of the heart. The line from the front left leg to the front right leg. The line from the liver of one ant to the liver of another ant. The straight line from earth to star #21436. The line from the eye of the boy who observes the ant to the ant to the eye of another boy who observes the same ant. The line from the anthill to the target food. The boundary between reason and investigation. The line from now to the big bang. The line, interior, from the thorax to the anus of the ant. The line from specie to specie. The line from love to fear. The line from animal to human. The ridiculous: the sublime. The boundary of one generation. The line from the thought of one person to the idea of species.

Somewhere and everywhere at a table made for a child on a chair made for a child a man sits writing. The line of ants moves toward its food, picks up minuscule bits of it, carries it back to the nest. The proportions between the size of the table and chair, the size of the man, the size of his writing, the ant, and the ant's morsel of food. The proportions between instinct and frivolity. The proportions between memory and presence. The proportions between the written and the unwritten. Were it not for the perpetual duration of the line of ants walking toward and back from its food the man could lose all perspective.

A man, tired from climbing, lies face down in the woods. In the mountains. He breathes, his body relaxes its strains. His chest expands, his stomach settles against the ground. His face turned to the side he inhales the fragrance of fresh sharp greens, brown dirt. His penis grows into the chest of the earth. Two holes open at his sides so that his arms reach down and around in an unimaginary embrace. To the east of him the line of ants travels northward. With eyes closed he is nonetheless minutely conscious of their movement. They do not change their course to surround him in one then two then tens then hundreds & thousands of concentric circles across the valleys and up the attendant mountainsides. When he sees the landscape entire covered with these concentrically encircled moving spheres of ants, the man takes one breath, withdraws his arms, his penis detumesces. He turns over. He looks up and into what he calls the sky.

He turns to the east. As the line of ants ascends as it descends over a hump in Earth they resemble the action of a wave: the apparently same matter moves in the same formation over the same space, while in apparent actuality always different matter moves over apparently actually different space in apparently actually different times. Soon water submerges the mountains and the valleys. With the power of his natural strength the man swims southward and westward then eastward and northward.

The delicacy as each foot of the ant touches ground. The perfection of the co-ordinated movement of the six legs.

The knowledge of a separation from a love for the things
of this life beginning with the relationship between the ant
and the hive that everyone must know of

Is an ant, with its lifespan of about two months, ever subject to migraine head-ache? nausea? neuralgia? cancer? ulcer? fever? plague? disorientation? exhaus-tion? backache? and of what do ants most commonly die? and where? and under what circumstance? and with what protocol? all these questions contin-ue under study by researchers who need to know the answers, scientists who already know that insect life achieves complex levels of order in response to threats from without, from the environment, from chaos.

Write a poem in which every stanza contains some reference to ants, to the life of ants, to the presence of ants. Why? Do not anthropomorphize. Do not met-aphorize. Stick to the facts.

A dryness. Soft but long. The ants remain in their lair. They stare. Above them a farmer walks alone among the things of his Earth recognizes his genius for un-derstanding is swept up in a joy which he nonetheless manages to absorb at the same time as he wonders how much this abrupt arousal of his understanding both universal and human has to do with the drought in which he walks.

Red ants. Black ants. Red red ants. Red red ants. Black ants. Red ants. Red ants. The movement of red of a red ant. The redness of a red ant. Red ant. Red red red ant. Deep red. Powerful intense red. Black ant. Red ant beside black ant. Make those ants stand still. Make the color colorate.

Obsess the ant. Dissect. Enlarge, hugely, until the eye sees. Enlarge all the world until the eye sees and seeing absorbs and into, is. The ant moves in slow motion. Observe the ant. See the ant. Say nothing about it. Watch the word ant move across the page. Watch the enlarged ant engorge the huge grain of salt. Exercise the world. Study the size of time. Write in enormous letters. Fall under the gaze of that which is greater than the universal. Turn out from the dream of the senses. Black. Red. Black black beside red.

In a moment of absolute ardor the ant crawls onto the sink of a suburban home. For twenty-seven years the residents have tried to annihilate this pest. When the ant returns annually they frustrate, but in laughing they rejoice so far beyond themselves they fear in their celebration even what appears to be their defeat. They move to another home. This is a true story – if you believe in true stories. It happened not long ago but in present time. It is not a myth. Not a legend. The ants appeared in their new home, where they had never infested before. This is not mythical nor metaphorical nor metaphysical nor does it suggest that the ants followed them, which is not possible and clearly not true. It is stupid. It is hysterical. It is beyond them.

At the head of the line of ants crossing the hayfields on ancient paths that stretch around the world the lead ant rolls in front of itself the imaginary ball.

Oh write without ants. Escape the ant in your art! Rise above ant! Write of love, of lovelessness, of lavishness, of laboriousness, of lability, of listlessness, of lassitude, of liberty, of latitude, of lust. But look at the ant! How escape the ant! Do not escape the ant! Do not rise! Above! Nothing! Antness and antlike is the antnessness of an ant even lost in the abandon of the lair.

The role of the ant can be arbitrary, but permanent. Once an ant, for no known reason, chooses (chooses) to be a sanitary ant, one who cleans inside or outside the colony, that ant maintains that task for life. Chance chooses. chooses chance ant. Impulse in chance. Enchanted. Choice. Becomes. Suddenly: does. Is. Is does. Arbitrary ant.

Infuriate the ant.

How many known species of ants are there? 20,000. How many unknown species of ants are there? 20,000? How do ants tell other ants where the food is? By leaving a trail of scent. How long do ants live? 45-60 days (a reliable or unreliable source has reported ants living from 9 months to 20 years). What is the Latin name of the slave-maker ant? Polyergus Rufescens. How do ants know if another ant comes from a different nest? Because of their unfamiliar smell. What is the name of the outer covering of an ant's body? The exoskeleton. How do the red ant species protect their nest? With a sting. What are the four stages of an ant's life? Egg, larva, pupa, adult. Why do some birds put ants in their feathers? To kill parasites. Where does the Ecitron Burchelli ant live? South America. How many stomachs do ants have? Two. Why? One for their own food, the other for carrying food back to the nest. Which type of ant steals eggs from other nests? Slave-maker. How many legs do ants have? Six. How many joints in each leg? Three. What do worker ants do with the colony's eggs at night? They take them deeper into the nest to protect them from the cold. What do worker ants do with the eggs at dawn? They bring them closer to the surface to expose them to the warmth. What kind of defensive acid do ants spray? Formic. If an ant were to weigh 2000 kilograms how much could it lift? 4,000 kilograms. Have ants inhabited Earth longer than homosapiens? Yes.

A man going out of his mind tears a leg from an ant. He tries to replace it.

Which type of Queen ant allows a foreign invader ant to drag her from her nest into the invader's nest where she bites off the head of the invader's Queen ant, then lays her own eggs in the foreign nest, forcing the worker ants of the now-enslaved foreign colony to care for her eggs? Bothriomyrmex.

Which type of ant drags the Bothriomyrmex Queen into their nest where, having bitten off the head of their Queen, she enslaves them? Tapinoma.

How many ants inhabit a nest? How long has ant inhabited earth? Do ants tire? Sleep? Do they prefer sun or shade? How do they decide when to construct a nest? Has any researcher ever distinguished two ants, one from the other? Have you ever watched and felt an ant crawl over your finger, your hand, out of curiosity,,,,, boredom,,,,, fascination,,,,, fatigue,,,,, distraction,,,,, even desire,,,,, in a state of bemusement,,,,, confounded at what the disparity in your relative size suggests about a world you inhabit, then either blown that ant off your wrist, or placed your hand on the ground so the ant might walk away?

All creatures participate in the action of the dimension, time, which began, which continues in linear expansion &/or circular motion &/or in a spiral whose arithmetic is incomplete and which is always the same everywhere and to each. Every stone. Each movement of an eye. In a landscape of eyes one ant.

> *I is an other*
>> Arthur Rimbaud

> *I does not exist*
>> Scroll of Taba
>> c. 100 C.E.

I am asleep in the Other's dream. In the flurry of an irrational clarity I know there would be no visions unless in its irrational clarity this may be that vision. In the Other's dream you wander the streets of the city in search of moments of being in search of an intensity you might be able to call life. This is the world without compromise or delusion. Even without intention. This is the real world. I walk through the city to the river upon which everycity is built so my eyes can open on the open space. I write in the water the word endurance and I write on the water the other word sunlight. In the Other's dream I am a coyote wandering the city streets until I find myself back in the underbrush loping through stands of liveoak and ancestors. And the Other follows me until I find myself in the Meadow of Song where one female soprano sings without cease day and night. And I follow the Other to the creek where drinking is mandatory from the singular waters. This is the world as it would be. This is the world as it could be. And as it is. I am no longer coyote. I am no longer in the city. I am the city. The city neither sleeps nor dreams. The city is awake, dreaming; the city dreams, awake. I awaken. The Other turns, releasing, spreading her dream throughout the room. As I leave her dream, she embraces me one last time. She calls me One because I have no other name. In her dream, she lights one candle. She calls it One. It burns inside the sleep that I sleep in the Other's dream. When I walk to where the table is set it's clear whether I'm walking in the dream or out of the dream of the Other, walking in my sleep or out of my sleep. When I arrive at the table I sit down with everyone. The music begins. All of the doors are opened – everyone coming in or going out. Some of them climb the last trail to the summit of the mountain. I am content with the view from where I am. Everything is simple. Everything is down to earth. The wine is made from the small vineyards right down the hill. You can see them from here. The tomatoes come from the garden on the other side. Over there. It seems like a holiday and I call you beautiful. When I rise to dance with the Other, the Other rises to dance with me. It is as if we had never heard of each other. It is as though any deceptions that may lie around us cannot blossom. Will not blossom. When, in the Other's dream of I, I fly off the mountain, I am protected by the winds even as I am exposed to the cold sun. I run through the winds. Until the Other follows me. She has to. It is an excruciating journey of stasis and arrivals. We enter the gates with triumphal joy. Here is the happiness the Other had dreamt of. In my sleep I eat. I was satiated. I awaken into the dream of the Other.

In Orange
     County
          California
   today
          a jury
       acquitted
       two County Sheriff's Deputies
          in the killing
of a homeless
          man. The man
              who suffered
       from a mental
            illness
       had a history
       of violence.
He was on
     the ground // pinned down
       by a cadre of six
          Sheriff's Deputies
            who beat him in the face
and head
     with the barrel
       of a tazer
       gun
          and with bare
          fists.
     The man

died

screaming: *Help me, help me, Dad! I can't breathe.*

While the original

autopsy

showed

the man

died of head

injuries

and asphyxiation

from the six officers'

crushing

his chest

a subsequent

autopsy

said

that he died

of heart

failure

for he had a history

of heart

problems

caused

probably

by his drug

abuse.

There are multiple layers of light.

Despite the death

of his wife

a year

earlier,

his birthday

celebration

was a lovely

event,

surrounded

as he was

by friends

and family
in the large
open
dining room
of a restaurant
where they were well
known
and warmly
welcomed.
Smiling,
he talked
for a minute
about how
surreal
it all
was.
But surrealism
was not
the goal
of the student
in a creative writing class
who turned in
a story
that had all and only
the elements
of so much

contemporary American media culture: a stream of violence made so bizarre, so vicious, so unredeemed as to make the audience laugh. Laughter, Freud and others tell us, is a release of pent-up, suppressed, prohibited emotions. When the suppressing force – society, family, super-ego – is cruel, then the humor is cruel and the laughter is explosive and itself ridden with cruelty. Can it be that our culture is so cruelly repressive? We hate to think so. Although, in mathematics, the beauty and simplicity of a formula can be the proof that its true. Just the beauty and simplicity! But that holds for aesthetics as well, doesn't it – that the beauty and simplicity of a language can be proof of its truth – truth in art being something altogether different than truth in mathematics. Truth in art is what emerges from the whole being of the artist and the whole being of the perceiver. That can be like unto Freud's theory of humor. Or his theory of art. The art (let's say, for example, the current James Turrell retrospective at LAC-MA) expresses what is sublimated—not repressed cruelly, unnecessarily—but, in this case, lightly, lightly repressed so we can function—the artificial light of Turrell's work fills us with an experience of light we can't every moment comprehend. It derives from our ordinary experience of life but heightens it. Which is not Freud's theory of art. Like language. Were—speaking of light—I to have written, above, "There are many levels of light" instead of "There are multiple layers of light," I would have used ordinary language to signify something out of the ordinary. A moment of exceptional perception, derived from but different than—ordinary perception. So there are different languages for different writing occasions.

alive

      in the under-
      world out
         for a walk
         in the sun

what we cannot
    know
      about
        we remain
   in ignorance.
        is ignorance
          a form
of love a form

of being
it
can be
                    it is not
a form
    of fear
            a form
of violence
            those
            are other things

the bright
            yellow
                    lemon
    fallen
        to the dewwet
                sun-
                        drenched
        bright   green
                        grass
                initiates
    the history
                of boredom
        as a co-efficient
                of the industrial
    revolution
                a language
        readable—or otherwise
conforms itself
                to these
                forms
        of what use
                        an unreadable
    language
                to a lemon to a

                grass to a
                                man
        to a
        woman
                        but
                        there
                        it is

BECAUSE OF SHIMON PEREZ

The only sacred language

      surprises that all languages

A rescue operation requires imagination

         the woman beside you
    is the woman inside you

           look: being itself
    is the surprise of the language
               that shapes this moment
               out of all the moments
               of history

    stand
         on the sea because only there

           do we feel the water how it carries the salt

        to the names of our tasting the common fig

      the extraordinary grape

           the pomegranate
some of them sold
         their birthright for the right

to be born they had to

       others indulged
            in a reality of peace until it was too late

       some of them agreed to the compromise between the music
                        and the silence

       there is no prison
       there is no acid
       there is nothing
       between the taste of seasalt
       and the return to the touch
       of distance
           touching distance oh
my softspoken speaker speak
       swiftly with softspoke place
       the generous heart in the community
       of solitude

            at the ceremony where the music where the song
immerses the distances
       put a gentle arm around the sea of space
     linger
       around the whirlwind

          the prophet speaks
      to the priestess
      in the way that you

          speak

to your lover / in the sand

before the weather changes
     the weather

has already
changed you
are the weather
the weather
is within you
the sea
the actual sea
is within you you
are
that sea
the hope of your brother
is your hope and you
are the hope of my brother
crossing the border
we are still
left looking at the other
side
though it's confusing
day
still follows
night air
still

breathes
the air
& the emptiness
so quickly fills
with things
with stone with airplanes with pomegranates
with smokestacks with bookstores with libraries with museums
with houses with flags with faces with memory personal
collective
geophysical with naked divas as they dance on the head of an
ear of corn
we rejoice we inaugurate
a holiday
we write
songs

on the instruments
that play them beginning
with the ram's horn

      & then the piano

and then the
drums
      that we hauled
            through the desert
   drying them out.

         outside of here
         is everywhere
inside of here
    is exactly contiguous
  with inside
        of here

    nothing
        tells us
  what to do everyone
  is chosen is a chosen
  person   every
            one
given
    the host
    of their names
        that will use them
        everyone
who must first
haul a drum
across the length
of a dream
to dry it out
all the realities
        of monday tuesday wednesday

so named
                by some god
so high the god
                of word-naming
i come home in the morning
                                i have eaten
                                the sun
i have planted a moon
into the sky
among all the stars
the planets
the satellites
the whorl
of universe
on multiverse

                                i listen
                to your words
                that rebalance
                the animal
                the vegetal
                the mineral
                the spiritual
                the corporeal
                the humane
                the inhumane

no one is choosing the no one who is not chosen we invest these days with imagination we imagine these days we close our letters with *love* we drink the cup of
water we rise to the footsteps that come toward us we know what is power we
know what is peace & what is peace of mind we hold that the tree of life and
the tree of knowledge have been ours to begin with we plant our gardens about
them we make walkways around them we know that we who are made are busy
making we doff our caps to one and another we argue about the details of the
minutiae of compassion we debate the minutiae of the details of if i am not for
myself who will be for me we choose even one of them said happiness the sun
never sets on our empire earth you put your hands into it they come up smelling

of sun we look at it from outer space it is the color of imagination we are not expelled from we walk out of the garden of eden carrying seed and soil we had to write about cain & abel we had to choose the myth of ourselves to become the main character connected ourselves a tale of love and fear of the olive tree the apartment building the sistine chapel the distance between the hand of god and the hand of adam we had to imagine ourselves the space of that distance in which we had to build the four-gated city in which by the force of imagination we walk out of one gate to circle to walk in by the next gate weaving a trail of dedication an air of kisses an imagination of the beautiful a never-turning turning of the other cheek a wedding party for the marriage of heaven and hell a poem of the death of the father the birth of the son

BECAUSE OF DONALD WILL

the angles of syncopation elevate

        the rhythms in the corridors of discourse

   here we go

        and here we go again

    holds trembling the hand

        to read the writing that scrolls the imagination

    you are the door

      that opens that closes you are

         the eye

           that looks

              into the eye

                that opens

                    that closes

down to the sea in ships we went

you and i and all the fellowships hopefully sublime

    you and i in front of history you

and any i not me but every i as you as well

      what might harm you and & any every i

dispel the spell say the word

      and here we are and here

and here

you are   no there you are

i cannot see you
holds it the eye beholds
again what
is a circle what
a triangle what
a parallelogram what
a kiss and what an arm
around a tender fiery world
at all

as an all am

to doing

as brazen acts

as fortitudes

on weepings
designated
here & there oh come

all you

now

open up the

fists our world

is made of
water : sun : sea
the nameless tune
of tide of alter contention

the titles of all

books read you
as a poem
down a page

yours the name
            to come
                        to comme to coming
and here
            we are
                        and here
   and here
                        and here and
            those
are the shoes you chose

                        to wear

      to wear walking

                        into the desert
& those

            the hands trembling
            you chose to take
                        arriving
                        inside the hours along the corridors

eye take you in
eye absorb you
eye just to see

                        you stand
                        on a cliff
                        look backward
                        look forward
                        look downward
                        look upward
                        look forward
                        & counting
                                    from one to one
                        & back again to one

let's talk
let's talk some more

        & here

          & here

let us name
all the animals
one
    by one

 by one

       together
          you & i & any i
          will spin the globe
          on its axis
          to the sun
             we'll
                    bear witness
              we'll hear the testimony we'll join

    the parade
    of smoke
       of elegance
        of eloquence
we will unname
       all the animals
        we will in/scribe

       inside the eye—we will erase
    we will erase
    we will erase
    we will erase
        we will in/scribe

the air
    is a force

that drives the divine
the sublime
& a death lies before you

as interesting as love

as dynamic as love

as bizarre as love

as necessary as love

as quintessential as love

as unanswerable as love

as invisible as love

as visible as love

as relevant as love

as irrelevant as love

as tolerable as love

as noisy as love

as driven as love

as aboriginal as love

as original as love

as chaotic as love

as far beyond language as is love

as passionate as love is

as irrational as non-commercial as love is

as daily as nonchalant as love

as lucky—as walt whitman says it is—as love is

as mysterious as birth is as love is

as unnameable as being is as love is

as much of a consciousness as love is

as non-intentional as love is

as urban as rural as suburban as love is

as much of a sign of life as love is
as much of a desire for life as love is

as possible as love is
as immoderate as love is
as excessive as love is
as unmitigated as love is
as without noise as love is
as much of today as of tomorrow as love must be
as much swimming in memory and desire is in memory as
   the absence of desire in desire as the end of memory
as profane as love is as harsh as love is
as kind as love is
as meaningful as love is
as *a priori* as love is as prior as primary as primitive
as electrical as chemical as shocking as love is
as much of water as love is
as ritualized as love is as ignorant
as noble as love is ennobling
as beyond mathematics as beyond equations as beyond
      the mechanisms of the mechanical as love is as
      sloppy as love is
as intelligent as much of genius as love is
as irreplaceable as love is
as full of yes and of no and the and as love may ever be
as fearful as fearsome as fearless as love is
as ecstatic as love is
as it is as imperfect as perfect as love is
as much an act of the imagination as love is

as much in need of itself returning to itself as love is

as complete in the form of incompleteness as love is

as fulfilling as love is

as disappointing as love is

as unbelievable as uncanny as love is

as incomprehensible as love is

as ungraspable as love is

as beyond our resistance as love is

as unending as love is

as nameable as love is

as shameless as love is

ii.

Witness the barricades witness the body
fecund the enemy fecund the ally the
best of times in the worst of times when
each one of us now chooses to know everything
from alphabets to shoelaces
from a lowly gnat to a glass of chardonnay
lift up a lovely face, my dear, lift all that you hold sacred
now's the loveliest hour come when gentle eyes open
homes are verdant & obscure & tantalizing
scattered everywhere everything known floats
everything a reckless freedom-seeking thing
to accept all constraints to bow down to eternity
as witness to potential energies inherent
in visionary atomic structures
we who had overcome the barricades who had crossed the lines.

iii.

desire creating desire
the atomic structure
of a howl
creating forms

and lovely lifted
between person / / to person
           between
   here
       & here
    & here
              &

BECAUSE OF TRISTAN TZARA

give the mind room to move
seep out the pours of the skull
let it float in the air
among the abundance of molecules
let it freshen the zones of the garden
let it shock the wings of the irregular zoëfly
let it breathe in the breathing night air
let it find turbulence on the horizon
then ride it to the end
of its death as its resurrection
let it expand through realms of precise chaos
let it discover the dew
that borders on hallucination
let it relax
under the shade
of the oliveladen tree
let it dream
once and for all
but an unfinished dream
that perpetuates the piazza empty
and the colonnade
let it wander let it expand so far
that it will never return
to the insult of the mere brain

i have gained all the spiritual wisdom i need
i have read enough books to last me yet another lifetime

i have told enough lies to condemn me to hell in a shrimp boat
i am the mother and the father of all the others i will ever know
you are the mother and the father of the only other i will ever know
i am the one who saved the infant from drowning in the bulrushes
i sit with him on the banks of the river
in the hard hard rain
waiting for the future to declare a truce

i declare that poetry – and the whole history of poetry—will come to an end at
    the end of this line
i am the one who created eternity it was a joke i was playing on some gods
    who came to irk me
i am the one who kissed you in the dark so many years ago just as you
    approached your puberty
i am the one who wrote the judeo-christian bible i take back every word of
    it none of it happened except the creation i wrote that then i got carried
    away
i am the one who threw Caution to the wind but then Caution threw me to the
    Ends of the Earth
i am the one who sold his genius for a shekel or two but then stole it back from
    the fool who paid so much for it
i am the superconductor who proved einstein wrong by proving einstein right
    i am the one who invented the zero and the passive verb the fiction of the
    verb to be i am not the *primum mobilum* – what? do you think i have that
    much pride that much hubris? but i did teach the *primum mobilum* to count
    to one
and i consider myself a very likeable person

WHY BUDAPEST

an elegy

the birds of Budapest lift they ground the
                                        off the all the
        ground at once

        to the upwarding gaze
of every budapestrian.

        the **MAYOR OF BUDAPEST**
                declares a festival.

                        the streets.
                                the squares.
                                        the bands.
                                                the colors.
                the sealed declarations unfurled
                in peace

                the **ARCHBISHOP**:
                        a miracle,
                                & he himself he pulls
                        the cords he rings
        the resonant the iron the clappered
        his bells of budapest oh my people we have finally
                have we
        a song to fill to fill the air

the **POET LAUREATE OF BUDAPEST**
          declares
                  in languages
                           the end
      of the *need*

for writingspeechthought
     she then begins
          a poem that begins

the **ASCETIC OF BUDAPEST** regrets his big action
           his wish:
                   to stand amidst / the rise /
                   from off that ground
                   of all the birds
                   of budapest
                   at once

         he rides a white
         hungarian horse
         in slow in noble gait
         around hero's square

         he knows by heart
         the thousand years old
         Declaration of the Air
         he hears it
         in his heart inclusive
         as round rides he
         slow
         as noble
         as horse
         as fly birds

the **DREAMER OF BUDAPEST** lets go himself
                                        into the darkness of the outlandish
                                hieratical dream
            by which his dream endarkens seeking darkformlessness

the **GENIUS OF BUDAPEST** projects maps
                                                charts
                                                        diagrams
                                                                graphs
                                                        schemata
                        to circle round onto the sides of buildings
                                        encircling university square
                            the maps
                                        the charts
                                                the diagrams
                                                        the graphs
                        the schemata that calculate
        just how
                all the birds

                of budapest

                might rise
                                        at once
                to show

                that what

                is happening

                is possible

                to show

                the mind

        an infinite space

of rehabilitations of reconciles
with reality with real reality so sometimes black
so sometimes green so at times a red or goldenrod so

the **DAMEON OF BUDAPEST** carries a little stick

around the corners of budapestrian streets tapping everyone
on the shoulder a lite budapestrian rap until
he's tapped
the shoulder
of every budapestrian
citizen
eye upskyseek the flight
of all the birds of Budapest
who fly who en whirl the buda pestrian firmament
blue

the **ALCHEMIST**
OF BUDAPEST discards stores
of spellspent chemical con-
coctions
to collect
the falling skyearth avian excrementa
to inaugurate
a century of electrical belief
to instigate the quest
for what is gravity
& what the emptiness
we hold aloft
in palms
upraised
that element
at the core
of element

the **TECHNICIAN OF BUDAPEST** records
—the flyflown screech

—those birds—within the flock—those dedicated to
　　　the highest register
　　　　　　in the deepest tone
　　　　　　　　of bodysong
　　　from which, with the **COMPOSER OF BUDAPEST**
　　　　　　　to build up hesitations
　　　　　to leaps of fate
　　　　　　　to shocks of sounds \ anew /
　　　　　　　　heard
　　　　　　　　　　　& unheard of
　　　　　　　　shocks of sounds : anew }

The **EXPLORER OF BUDAPEST** turns attention homeward
to the ground of disbelief to the ancestry of his discontent
to the gate of his desire in that paradoxical paradise
　　　　　　　　to remember
　　　　　　　　the origins
　　　　of the arts of navigation
　　　　into unknowns of sacrifice
　　　　toolless ,,,,, clueless

　　　　to forget his discovery
　　　　of the number one
　　　　　　to discover his discovery
　　　　　　　　of the power of zero
　　　　　　　　to make

the **GARDENER OF BUDAPEST** listens to the plants
the flowers the leaves the seeds the eighty-nine species
of the animals of the underground
awhole amongst themselves in their
budapestrian dialect of birth of growth of death of birth
of growth of death as nonsequential conundrums outside
the realms of joy of grief inside the realms of joy of grief
churn the earth awhole the sun

the **CARTOGRAPHER OF BUDAPEST** cartographs the homography
of spacetimegravity he wants to sign his name
on the map of at least one alternate universe
he yearns to do so and not for fame alone
he reaches his hand out of his hand

the **HEALER OF BUDAPEST**
        paints all scars red
    with a red pencil
        he draws out the living from the voices of the dead
not as prophecy but as the ode:
            The Landing of the Birds of Budapest
            Past Midnight and Beyond
            as Witnessed By the Lamplighter Alone
            While its Citizens Sleep
            While the City Revels
            in Ambuiguities of Solitude
            in a Fulgation of its Aviarium Amen

DIFFERENCE

the difference between an ellipse and a parabola is that one is a man standing in the rain the other is a woman standing in the shadow of a triangle

the difference between an ellipse and a parabola is the distance resulting from the tri-root of the psychic relationship between the formal gardens at versailles and the michelangelo gardens whose wilder waves michelangelo rides throughout umbria

the difference between the ellipse and the parabola is equal to the quadrant reaction between what we call the imagination and what we so lovingly call the real

the difference between the ellipse and the parabola is that where the ellipse crosses the parabola the function is zero whereas where the parabola crosses the ellipse the function is incalculable

the difference between the ellipse and the parabola is equal to one-sixteenth of the quotient of the constant of laughter in the universe and the constant of weeping in the universe divided by the equivalence factor of incertitude times the substance of pure being as measured on the bimodal scale of equivalized subjectivity

the difference between the ellipse and the parabola is the same as the difference between the Alexander's Queen butterfly and the dung beetle the difference between the ellipse and the parabola is the difference between wisdom and ignorance in a spin of perpetual exchange of one for the other the ellipse for the parabola the parabola for the ellipse

the difference between the ellipse and the parabola is the difference between the expected and the sublime between the alpharoot and the political harangue between the truth and the annual snowfall in the hinterlands

the difference between the ellipse and the parabola is the difference between the hand and the mind between the body and the being between that consciousness which is not those images that pass through our mind's eye as we call it that do not come in directly through the eye but remain as memory and the difference and the distance between the person who has a memory and the person who is the subject of the memory

the difference between the ellipse and the parabola is the difference between night and day i.e. it is relative to where you stand to where an angel stands on the head of a pin

the difference between the ellipse and the parabola is the difference between victory and defeat in the repetitive wars of nations even the internecine wars of nations even brother-against-brother but not the same as that negotiation between self and other even when self might be an other

the difference between the ellipse and the parabola is the difference in the rise of the crescendo to an overwhelming to an absolutely necessary height to a moment of enlightenment to a moment of tears of release to a nearly unbearable sense of awe of emptiness of renewal at which the audience wants to but restrains itself from crying out and the bow of the conductor of this invisible orchestra

the ellipse is the ellipse and the parabola is the parabola and while they may cross they will never meet—a source of awe in the world of geometry in the world of radio broadcasts in the world of wine the difference between the ellipse and the parabola is that of the differentiation between the lightness of chaos and confusion and the weight of chaos and con-fusion a slight but enormous distinction

the difference between ellipse and parabola is the distance between is and was is the distance between is not and never was is the distance between will be and will be

the difference between ellipse and parabola is the difference between hydrogen and selenium between soil and rock between diamond and jordanite between carrot and pineapple between ant and anthracite between fire and smoke is the difference in number in weight in structure and we believe even in purpose leaving laid bare the difference in meaning

the difference between ellipse and parabola is the difference between the raw and the cooked between the natural and the manmade the discovered and the created the origin and the repetition the desire and the fulfillment the project and the map the map and the compass the water and the air

the difference between the ellipse and the parabola is the difference between the beginning of the journey and the continuum of the going

the difference between the ellipse and the parabola is the difference between the calculation of the distance from one galaxy to the next and the calculation of the distance from one person to the next

the difference between the ellipse and the parabola is the subject for discussion among a group of people sitting around a table engaged in a conversation of passing words from one to the next then around and back again transformed into the equation that solves the question of fate as a function of amor fati and as the coefficient of the sum of the beautiful and the cruel.

AND WHAT IS MEMOIR

We sat in a restaurant—outdoors—it was in Florence. Crowds ran by us toward the river. There were fireworks over the Arno. Some occasion. There are always festivals in Italy. I got up. "Let's go!" I said. "I don't care about fireworks," you said. But I insisted, and we went. We stood in the crowd. The fireworks were professional, an extraordinary display. The crowd—so Italian—sang out bravo! over and over, after each explosion. It was an opera. We never made it to La Scala, which has no summer season. Why am I writing this? What is the value of memory? *The Persistence of Memory,* Salvador Dalí paints. Yet, memory always changes. It is not the same experience as what happened. And, memory remembers correctly or distortedly. And, as we remember, we live in the present, that present which is more significant than the past. The past is a myth, a mythos by which we make the present. With which we make the present. We were happy in the way that we can remember remembering happiness in order to support to affirm to enliven to prove the happiness of the present. But why do I write this? So often this memory passes through my consciousness, yet, now, I want to capture the words that memory evokes. This writing is not so much about the memory as it is about the writing. Is all writing in a sense a form of the wording of memory. Even a fictional memory, even a fiction which becomes a memory. This writing is about the essentiality of writing. I disagree with Wordsworth that writing is an act of the "the overflow of powerful feelings: it takes its origin from emotion recollected in tranquility." The act of writing is not tranquil. Any more than the act of painting or of musical composition is tranquil. It is all—as Clement Greenberg said of Jackson Pollock—*action*—action painting, active composing, active writing. The power of emotion enacted for *the sake of* painting, composing, writing. So the memory of our day in Florence—so vivid in my mind – is a spur to the writing. It is not an inspiration for the writing it is a vehicle for the writing. Writing itself is the inspiration.

But, what is the inspiration, the act of writing? Is it the pressure of words, of language itself, to act—through us? There is a saying from the Mwindo of Africa: If a story—which wants to be told—is not told—it will take revenge. If there is a language that wants to be written—it must be written. And it is not just the words—the specific words—that want to be written, but *language itself* (whatever that is—the impulse in the body in the brain) that wants to be written. The words, too, are a vehicle.

Nietzsche writes that all art begins as an impulse in the body. I long ago concluded from this that language is already a metaphor for that impulse in the body. So that good writing (good music, good painting, good dance, good architecture, good film) arouses that impulse in the body of the audience. So that art is the arousal of impulse, in the author, the creator, and the audience. Thus, there is no difference between them, between the creator and the perceiver. So when we talk about language, we aren't talking about words or grammar. We're talking about that instinct in the body. What you are reading now is a communication of energy to energy.

That's why I have said that art is energy. That energy is achieved by disrupting the normative art form, which creates fissures in the form along which the energy travels and along which the audience achieves, accomplishes, perceives it, receives and transforms it. The more powerful the disruption, the stronger the energy. This does not mean that any disruption, each such disruption can accomplish this. It must be strong. It must originate *and be most directly* transposed from that impulse in the body.

I have also called this the Chaos Theory of Literary Composition (as a prescript, for example, to my *Subset of Chance*. [Lillebulae]). [In physics, Chaos Theory describes the phenomenon of energy (fire, flame, heat) applied to matter (water [for example]). That doesn't mean that it's all just chaos. That means that the composition must undergo a period of turbulence. [In the Chaos Theory of physics, energy (fire, flame, heat) applied to matter (water [for example)) causes turbulence, causes disruption in the form of that matter. The water boils. This chaos state *reveals* new form.] In art, in writing: passion, intelligence, vision, imagination, intuition provide the heat that causes the disruption. New form is revealed.

And what is memoir?

GREAT WIND

the great wind blows the united states close to africa it blows the eiffel tower
to berlin it blows japan off the map toward venus it blows the united nations
building to an island in the pacific it blows your house to where you have always
wanted to be no changing your mind now it blows hong kong to brasil resulting
in the formation of a new language and a new cuisine the great wind it blows
the mind open it blows the whales of the sea on a furious course around the
world's oceans it blows the remaining glaciers of the north further north so they
freeze more and more water and water the great wind it blows everything into a
stillness it blows harlem new york a hundred years back into its history it blows
across the battlefields of the american civil war across fort sumpter across get-
tysburg raising the voices of lincoln and robert e. lee so that we hear them sing
the national anthem the great hymn of the republic it blows open the curtain
of truth we see behind it we are laughing at the great blue the great red the
great yellow the grey the white the green wind the great wind blows israel back
to jesus christ to moses to braham and sarah and beyond to some solitary bed-
ouin shepherd asleep under an olive tree blown away it blows the atmospheric
traces of the bomb at nagasaki to los alamos we must invent a counterwind the
great wind it blows napoleon's army right up against that of alexander the great
right up against that of genghis kahn what the hell will happen now the kaiser
is smoking his cigar the wind blows in as a message in sanskrit something about
eternity something about a harmony of the spheres something about the skirt
of a lady and the name of a dog the great wind it whips up storms of children
howling for freedom and finding it and howling for more it throws the valleys
of hell up into the pastures of heaven where the oppositions create the greatest

works of art of music of poesia ever known to the universe of wind the great wind it blows me to you him to her us to them we to i it blows the taj mahal to the middle of the great lakes it blows the cover off your consciousness it blows the crown jewels to the slums of soweto the children frolic with them it blows the birds of paradise through the air they are flying flying it blows the american eagle to the moon it blows the crow to crowing enormously it blows the great wind blows all the world's money to the winds no one can grab it it blows through the hands it levels the ural mountains leaving europe staring at asia staring back at europe exposed now for its true love of beauty of bestiality i mean europe no i mean asia the great wind breaks windows especially the stained glass windows of the vatican and the great marc chagall's the great wind breathe it in sleep with it awaken within it dream it know it could be a nightmare it could be a balm it could be a great joke of a wind that won't quit joking with us with its little world it loves to play with.

FACES THE

in the mirror
                  that faces the mirror
                                that faces
      the mirror that faces themirror

the object—say the brooch found in an antique jewelry store—

      that had been brought from eastern europe
      over a hundred years ago by someone's great
      grandmother

is—in each mirror within each mirror—a different object

      that it does not add up
      to one whole

      that it adds out
      in the same way
            that it subtracts
            inwardly

      until one sees what one thinks of
      as an illumination

GARDEN

The irrational tree breaks the surface of glass. It is obvious that the past has no bearing on the seed. The politician is not lying! Be wary of identities formed in mirrors of stone. Only liquids flow. Where climate change will take us no one can imagine. The father tells the son that if he can imagine something it can come to be. All his life the son tests this dictum against the knowledge embedded in energy equals the speed of light squared. Absorb what frightens you, the son tells the daughter—become your disappointments and you will awaken from sleep one day as if you have no need to know what are the great questions.

A DIALOGUE   AN INQUIRY
A MORNING A DAY A NIGHT

        sacred that
    which was lost to be found
    in the annals of the torn dream
in order
    to be lost again until found
        in the certainty of a face
      turned in to face the heat to be cleansed
    of heat
sacred that
    which was lost to be found
    in the architecture of the ancients
in the ordinary procedures of their washing habits and weightless

      the presence of the automobile
    in the arc of history

       & weightless
    the denominations of moneybills
in the hands
      of high rollers
    weightless the audience
at the performance of The Trojan Women
    two thousand five hundred years ago weightless
      what should have been and was not or what
    was and should not have been weightless
the gold ring on the hand of the sycophant
      sacred the birth or the rebirth

of an ignorance infused
        with an innocence derived
     from the essence of the wordpetal
          wet   still

                from the passing rain
                sacred
                the event of anti-matter
                in the universe of reason
                as it moves past
   the speed of light

sacred

     the speed of light

   sacred
       the baseball bats of october
    a thousand of them
  hang from the sky
     & sacred
the appearance of the sacred
   among the coffee cups
     & the ferris wheels
  of molecular identity
& sacred
    the automobiles
  of the human imagination
      and its tender nightmares
    & sacred
        is the hilarious image
    of the magic penis and the magical vagina & sacred sacred
  is the permeable wall between being and non-being crossed all day
    long
  by the atoms of the invention of the selfcreatorinitself
weightless is the teacher and weightless the student and weightless
is the classroom that evolves into laughter

& sacred is the love that leads you where you deigned to go to discover
    love's almighty
struggle to say with him look! we have touched the body of our bodies have
    gone beyond the limits
of the human to be the human to kiss at midnight what calls for us
                & sacred is the telephone
                    & sacred is the lightbulb
                        & sacred is the doorknob
and weightless weightless
are the memories of underdevelopment
                weightless the discovery of unnameable meaning
                    achieved at the cellular
levels of philosophies
              & weightless the word of the man who talks of self-expression
              and the man who demands of him what
                          self what
                self are you speaking of speak speak of selves and
                other things such as derricks andmarine animals
                aswim in the midst of fieldclouds   speak

                of friendships of crises of meaning speak of the
                  speed
                        of change in the human time
            speak
              of the television set speak
            of the inertia of outer space
        speak
        of something
        you know about speak
        of 2 plus two & of how
we arrived there and then

        speak of the sacred
        of the weightless
        in the same breath
        of air

PENELÓPE

Penelópé here you are at your loom immersed in the darkness unweaving your day's woven narrative of cloth. Here you are at the wars of time of desire of chaos. So that each day's labor dissolves into the end of the beginning. Penelópé here you are careful not to unweave your fingers in the process down to the blood down to the bone. And how does a woman, how does a wife and a mother a queen sustain meaning in the midst of this lie of the unwoven. How does a woman a mother a queen come to love the lie come to call it truth come to love it so much that it is no longer a lie but a reality so unqualified so unmitigated so inaccessible to the investigations of so irrelevant of truth a reality lived and living. Without the unweaving there would be no truth. You Penelópé you know that the very existence of Greece, incipient Greece depends—not on the weaving—but on the unweaving—it is itself the only heroic truth of Greece. Why? Because it is the unweaving of your—Penelópé's—imagination, which becomes the very landscape of Ithaca of Hellas of Ἑλλάς of Greece. Why? Because it is the unweaving of your—Penelópé's— imagination wherein becomes the very landscape of Greece the rock of it the soil of it the tree of it the land of it its seaform. And all of this so that this Greece this polis this nation this state of mythos can inspire you, Penelópé, at your loom, immersed in this darkness unweaving each day of Odysseus.

So that is why, when Odysseus arrives in the royal castle of Ithaca dressed as a beggar, why, when you see him and know him and wonder at what a rag-tag figure to whom you had dedicated a life of waiting, wearing you down. Because the truth of this truth of this lie is that the hundred suitors are not

Odysseus's rivals. His one rival is all those nights of solitudinous unweaving in which Penelópé alone created the Greece capable of creating Penelópé-the-weaver. For her to accept Odysseus is to sacrifice the future of those evenings for the far more simple far more ordinary life of the man Odysseus. Woven the mortal man Odysseus. For Penelópé had woven and unwoven—on her loom—mortality and immortality.

To come home, Odysseus has sacrificed the gift of immortality, he has sacrificed the nirvana of the Sirens, he has sacrificed the adventure—albeit the hardship —of a life of wandering which he knows will inscribe his name in the poesia of Greece and the world.

Yet Penelópé makes the greater sacrifice. She sacrifices the act of unweaving. She sacrifices her imagination. Yet her reward is the greater. For from the sacrifice of her imagination, Penelópé knows will come Oedipus and the Trojan Women, will come Heraclitus and Aristotle, will come Pindar and Sappho, will come the Emperor Augustus and the Aeneid of Virgil, will come Jesus Christ and St Paul the Apostle, will come the Slavic invasion the Franks the Venetians, will come the homecoming of Greeks to Greece, will come the Ottoman Turk, will come independence and the wars and the wars and the fascists and "not the Greeks who fight like heroes but the heroes who fight like Greeks," will come the Communists the Democracies will come up James Joyce to reap from the loom of the solitudinous unweaving of the cloth of Penelópé of the imagination of Penelópé will come Stephen GreekDaedalus and Mr. and Mrs. Leopold and Molly Bloom of GreeceIreland. Will come even the predecessors of unweaving Penelópé Chronos and Gaia will come Athena and Zeus and Orpheus and Eurydice and even the Underworld and will come also this very day itself of the 15 November in the Christian year Two Thousand Fourteen with all of its mythos of truth and lie of the journey of life heroic tragic comical lost and found and musical as played on the modern lyre.

SEXTAIN IN E MAJOR

the difference between a bird and a man is
that a bird can be a man but a man cannot be a bird
the difference between an orange and an orange is an orange
a paradise of time is within you
in the continuum of lightning bolts the issues of the day are resolved
the earth is at rest the earth is always at rest

IDENTITY / POLIS

sunspot on blue / shadow on green: there is no mistaken identity there is no mistaking the identity of the sleeping woman who falls asleep angry who will wake up agreeing to the daylight reveling in the tree and the chair and the somersaulting ballet dancer—there is no mistaking the identity of agriculture invented 10,000 years ago and the invention of the television and the telescope and the human voice but it is possible to confuse the identity of jerusalem or new york possible to confuse the identity of the chaos machine to confuse the identity of a sunspot on royal blue to confuse the eye to confuse the mountain to confuse the musical composition to confuse the sound of the lion to confuse the desert to confuse the organization but it is not possible it is not possible to confuse the circle the triangle or the eponymous parallelogram

GEOLOGY OF HOURS

the age of the universe is irrelevant
the water is flowing
       & the water is flowing
the day opens
it is a woman's body
hidden behind reality

1897

lo: last night i dreamt that israel was at peace not just with our neighbors but with herself

la: amazing what these words can do how they ride the light

lo: so different than the israel we've yet to know

la: words aren't symbols of anything yet look at all the rambunctious stuff that they do that they get themselves into

IRAN DOMINATES OBAMA-NETANYAHU MEETING

lo: all israelis would be different because of this peace i dreamt of

la: and yet where do they come from all these words we know i'd love to just once see where they come from that wordless origin wouldn't that be something

lo: because as he'd said we haven't been afraid to make war and we are not afraid to make peace

2011 BRINGS PROMISE TO STOCKS WITH HIGH-DIVIDEND YIELDS

la: like the words is & is not don't all words contain their opposites because of where they come from. or that the words suggest oppositions or the unifying of oppositions or suggest meanings where you can't quite see the meaning like in the medieval jerusalem mystic reuven who wrote that "only the void fulfills the emptiness"

lo: my father told me—we were sitting in jerusalem—at a jewish café—that my father's lebanese friend—from beirut—signed all his letters to my father with the arabic salutation: infinite bliss. do you think such a thing exists, my father asked me? a bliss that is infinite? and can it co-exist with the stream of the extraordinary ordinary of things within that stream? or are those just meaningless words —*infinite bliss*? if the temple were rebuilt from the western wall would there be a reign of infinite bliss? and yet isn't bliss infinite as long as it lasts? is the universe —as one of the rabbis of the first temple once said—always in a state of infinite bliss? and aren't we—as the same rabbi said—the supplications of that bliss?

la: and then just think about how a language forms the way we think for example if i say the word father what do *i* think of and what do *you* think of? and all from just one little word

lo: and why did i have that dream i had to ask myself. i had it because i so want that peace i want it so and i didn't even know how much i wanted it until i dreamt my want my desire my outrageous demand my childish tantrum

PRIME MINISTER: ISRAEL HAS ACTED AGAINST U.S. ADVICE BEFORE

la: have you ever seen a word arrive and be and then depart i mean literally well i mean in your mind seen a word arrive in a somewhat unformed unshaped way and then become the word *here* and then depart again into dissolution. have you ever? no? have you never? they arrive like annunciations but of what what of? i'm just a little nutty aren't i?

lo: and i don't just mean a cold peace i mean where all the arab states felt friendly toward israel and israel felt friendly toward all the arab states and what wouldn't all that be like, huh? well i'm not crazy i'm just saying it was my dream. i'm not naïve. i'm not outside the pale of passions outside the aether of innocuous rages

la: did you know that carl gustav jung told james joyce: james, he said, jimmy, boy, he said, your schizophrenic daughter lucia she is drowning in in the seas that you james joyce that you swim in meaning of course the seas of language freed from what? freed from language's normative role of meaning only one thing in only one way at only one time

lo: once, i was walking in haifa with two friends: one israeli and one palestinian. i said to them both: think of the word israeli what comes to mind and then think of the word palestinian what comes to mind and you know what they both said about both words: an enigma they said. about both those words. and that's what they were calling *themselves*

TAX CHANGES FOR NEW IMMIGRANTS

la: look. the moon now is rising. i mean the sun now is rising. look. there. do we call that the sun or the moon?

lo: in a turkish café in jerusalem he said to me: whoever owns jerusalem owns the world & i said i own jerusalem it's a city full of ancient languages of quarried beliefs & their disbeliefs of predestined harmonies even of flying carpets for sale of maggots feeding on stone & marble of shades resisting people of poetries elevating fig trees to the level of foremothers of tourists looking for modern jewish prostitutes who might whisper magical signs

la: there are the languages of magical signage to be found in the medieval gardens of italy & spain but their symbols are so far indiscernible although i know what they say would you like to know what they say? no? ok. of course not

lo: i'm going to repeat it: israel at peace not only with her neighbors but with herself. golden hospitals. a nobel prize in every home. A cool wind along the axis of fervencies. an israel that exists and will exist that resides in the plethora of its existence & its non-existence

INTERNATIONAL ATOMIC ENERGY AGENCY CHIEF: IRAN NOT TELLING ABOUT NUCLEAR PROGRAM

la: is there a difference between the words existence & non-existence? what does kabbala say? what does st. augstine say? what does the poet say the one who couldn't be stopped from digging with his shovel in the vineyards looking for the potsherds of his family's demise

lo: i mean also her neighbors at peace with israel and at peace with themselves

la: the languages are all inexhaustible even were someone to try to exhaust them

lo: only the country—israel—herself is real: jerusalem, tel aviv, haifa, jaffe, the hills of judea, the white white moonscape drive along the road to the dead sea, the kids in the streets of acre, the garbage truck, the #7 bus, the finest falafel of homegrown labor and adolescent daydreams at the stand on the hilltop right where the jewish the armenian the christian and the muslim quarters converge to the sound of the music of the fishes

A RAPIST REDUCED TO BLAMING THE COURTS

la: *if* we agree that language can't arrive at what was once called truth & that what language *can do* is describe the world word by word then what does it mean if i say: the lord is my shepherd or the woman is not a woman but an image come naked from the garden of shamelessness to imitate our world or the sun stood still over jericho or the ship gallops over the rooftops of that neighborhood night after skyseed or if i say they listened to the music from where they had once gone inside the radio sound wave

lo: perhaps despite appearances every man woman & child in the land of israel is at their core driven by a precise logic which one scholar said was the first gift given by yahweh to moses on sinai. that scholar climbed sinai. her mind clarified with a precise impulsive logic that includes the proposition: israel exists and it does not exist *la*: the basis of language is logic; the basis of logic is grammar: the logic of grammar is beauty; the grammar of beauty is the midnight of existence

lo: the two pilgrims—one arab the other a jew—approach the temple mount and the western wall. with a kind of indifference found only in the sublime two security police approach each pilgrim, accept their passports as valid, then grant each one leave to proceed. These two will never meet. If they did, how would they describe how would they discuss how would they express their respective experiences to each other? think about it. If the time came and the circumstances were right they would kill each other

ISRAEL CALLS ON UNITED NATIONS TO CONDEMN ROCKET ATTACKS FROM GAZA

la: the israeli philosopher ben ezra writes: as we now know, when everyone, as a child, looks into a mirror at a certain moment and sees for the first time "themself" they hear that voice that speaks to them as themself, doesn't a nation or a people also have such a moment? but what if, at a certain point in time much later, that nation sees that the voice of itself which speaks to itself falls away, grows faint and quiet. what is left? is it something altogether new which had always been there? ben ezra went on to say that this could have been a question for kabbalah. after all, it's a question of language in which the letters fall away. after that ben ezra wrote no more philosophy but enjoyed—every bit as he had enjoyed philosophy—a second career as a botanist specializing in the breeding of and revolutionary methods of cultivation of roses and especially of succulent roses that would grow in the desert where he'd settled

lo: the breeze blew through the garden of roses bearing scents from africa

la: i call you by every conceivable name ad infinitum and i hear you answer. i begin from the beginning i continue without bitterness

lo: the grammar of wheat incites the scream of experience

JUSTIN BEIBER AND ISRAEL'S MISSED OPPORTUNITY

la: my notebook was new, the pages were empty. i could have read a book. instead i went out for a walk looking for words. i found thousands of them. & hundreds of thousands

lo: i suddenly was hungry for sights to fill my eyes. i walked out among all the buildings. i walked through the streets. i walked all the way to the beach then all the way back home. it was exhilarating. all that time i was no one i was all of no one

la: if you wait long enough the right word will come to you. this could take minutes hours days or years. you might not know the right word for what you want until a long time after you begin searching. but it'll come. even if you have to make it up it'll come. every word has an urge to come

lo: when i realized that i had a competition going with all my male friends i wondered if that weren't a kind of madness. not that i didn't love some of them all of them. but i had to ask myself what was this competition? what was i competing for? when the best thing i could get was friendship. i went around to all my male friends with a different thought in mind and goddamn it it worked. the competitiveness fell away. i lost nothing. i was more attached to everything even my country which for god's sake i'd fought for even having watched some of my friends with whom i'd been competitive fall in battle

IDF: WE ARE READY FOR POSSIBLE MILITARY OPERATION IN GAZA

la: we say friendship what do we mean. when we say love what do we mean. when we say self what do we mean. when we say enemy what does it mean. all these words mean something important

lo: and then i got to thinking about my country. looking around me, everyone i saw was a countryman/woman. i thought of them as fellow countrymen. man woman and child. even dogs! that's the way thought is. that's an israeli dog. isn't that crazy. even people i mean israeli strangers whom i might see on the street and have no personal affinity even vast differences with i think of as country-men/women. israeli arabs—they're countrymen. druze—they're countrymen. the super orthodox from whom i also am alienated—they're countrymen/wom-en. a thief, a prostitute, even a lawyer! yet what is it i share with these people that i don't share with others of a different even a friendly country who are also dif-ferent from myself. from the most ancient of times all this means something and you can't escape it. even if you go somewhere to find out who you are outside that country you come from somewhere as alien to your culture as you might get somewhere like india, say. it wouldn't change a thing. it can't

la: in the tensionspace being erases nothingness act on the first miracle of a god-given language to a bookbody people

lo: we are a stoneborne bookbound bookenamored booklost mesmerized peo-ple of the sacred parchment whose fires ignite our synapses we who are the contemporary kind of freethinkers liberated from the book in quest of the trans-lucent book

lo: the grammatology of sex walk the desert granulated earth to cools underfoot step calculated in terms negotiated under the sign of the broken egg under the aegis of a breathless tribe inventing geometric proportions between then and now between the here and the there the geometries of the brain to the respon-sibility owed to the heritage of poets

A TWO-LEGGED GREAT DANE

la: someone once said that without language we live in a world only of a con-tinuous continuum one thing melding without meaning into another. it's only language that gives us any chance at order at functioning at doing at being. but i don't quite believe that. something prior something more instinctual gives us all of that; *then* language comes along to name it. language lets us communicate it. language allows us to say: "i'll meet you at the cave at noon." but i have carved out the meaning of a cave and i know the sun before we had named it sun. where in the mind does all that take place. or, in the whole body

lo: and then i think well the legends abraham sarah isaac rebekah jacob leah they're all countrymen whom i never knew but they mean something so much different than what george washington means to me. king david. solomon. even i have no idea of who king david or king solomon were. what muhammad means to a muslim. what odysseus means to a greek. and i build myself on that. i can't help it. jesus christ is an interesting case. he was born in my country he died in my country. but to me he's not a countryman. that's what they've done to him. that's how strange strangeness is, otherness is

la: it's nighttime. it's just turned night. elephants lumber across the sky. the night signals to the cartographers. the false gods turn over their names to the dispenser of names. lives there a true god who keeps the name? such a ridiculous question I won't even grace it with an answer

lo: take passover, for example. archeologists here have concluded that the exodus from egypt never happened. they have a whole nother story about how the jews came from Egypt and it's wholly different. no thousands ever came. and every year we sit around a table and we eat certain foods and we say certain ritual sayings and we interpret the stories and we talk about freedom from all kinds of slavery and it all none of it ever happened. and i love that. it fills a void while leaving the void a void. and it is all about spring yet we cannot talk about spring as a void spring happens. spring is. spring belongs to no one. no one makes it happen. there is no moses of spring. spring is an unalterable fact of being like being human is unalterable. so i think of passover as a ritual of being human. no one else does but then everyone invents their own judaism. even if you have to destroy a myth to do so. i am all for certain kinds of destruction. it's the only way to get anywhere when there is nowhere to get to but here

ISRAELI AIR FORCE STRIKES GAZA TARGETS AFTER ROCKETS FIRED AT BEER-SHEBA

la: in the tensionspace nothingness devours being a god-given miracle of revelation to a people in love with time who celebrate the turn of each season with the corn with the wine wrought forth from the covenant with the seed-mystery

lo: say that this is the last moment you had on earth to say something entirely earthly. would you say that the whatever of death is nothing compared to the grandeur of living? the grandeur of the incomprehensibility of living. would you say that the question of living is grander than the ineffability of dying. would you say that even after this moment your greedsoul would cling to the living until it yields up its sacrilegious its devout envy its grandeurpassion. would you say that everything worth saying must be said even the most worthless the most vain prayer uttered in the fragments of the templestones parched of legends absent of myths the most altruistic flowering absurd song of itself

la: so. we have to take up this question. it was supposed to be "what is a jew?" but now it's become "what is here?" it's gone from a possible question to an nonsense question. a question that has abandoned the senses. is that the transition the transformation from talmud to kabbalah? from jesus christ to st. augustine? from shakespeare to beckett? from what you were to what you are? to what you are not? so then: what is "are" and what is "are not"?

TRANSGENDER WOMAN DENIED ACCESS TO WESTERN WALL

lo: he holds *the will to change* in the palm of his drained out breath. it capitulates to the trembling that comes from the river. it resides in the miracle that we call the oscillations of the nerve ends. the trembling of *the will to change* recapitulates the birth of the womb. the stasis of pure action is a bloodtrust bridge to the stasis of pure thought from the perpetuum that illuminates the spectrum of light

la: the equation is also a form of words which defines a reality. there was once an equation of grain and an equation of the fortifications for the heart *lo*: and i've taken up a history of the equations of the middle east and i've drawn a series of equations of the middle east all of which include in them equations of the cosmos because everything is related to everything and because you can't describe a utopia without describing the struggle to achieve it without describing the history – in immutable equations – of the success of utopias

AND THE FORECAST IS….HOT!

la: is it possible to draw an equation of the mind?

lo: it's possible to construct an equation of the history of the mind

la: the individual mind or the history of mind itself?

lo: isn't it im/possible to differentiate an equation of the landscape from an equation of the mind. doesn't every equation of a landscape signal an equation of the mind. an equation of wishes. an equation of detritus. an equation of knowing. an equation of personal objects

UNITED STATES ATTACKS TALIBAN-HELD AFGHAN TOWN

la: isn't every equation a book whose narration is finally pinned fully to the page and whose formulation has to be rewritten continuously

lo: here in the middle east we say the equation changes every ten minutes

la: even the name middle east is an equation. the equation is always asking: where am i/who am i

DANCE REVIEW: AVI GOTHEINER

lo: the equation is always asking: what is change what is chaos what is the equation of the irrational *la*: what might ever formulate the equation of the distance between us, between you and i.

lo: is there a distance between us, between you and i

la: it depends on how you read the equation

FATAH ACUSSES IRAN OF TRYING TO BLOCK PALESTINIAN UNITY

lo: you need an equation to define what you are and where your enemies are

la: you need an equation to calculate that which lies at the heart of equation: the garden of eden

lo: an equation of delusions.

la: an equation of the odors of seeing

CAN SHE LEAD?

lo: an equation of sleep

la: an equation of oppositions

lo: at the heart of the same equation, then, there is gehenna, there is hell which is the garden of discord which is the anguish generated in the dissolution of ash into hate an inextinguishable flood remorseless in acid

la: an equation of human energy

THREE NEO-NAZI PARATROOPERS SUSPECTED IN FRENCH SHOOTING

lo: an equation of energy itself

la: an equation of the human condition. doesn't every human have her/his own condition? make her/his own condition? *know* her/his own condition

lo: i have seen written the equation of the leagues of friendship

la: have you ever seen written the equation of the sensibility of the heart

FOR PALESTINIANS, NON-VIOLENCE PAVES THE PATH TO STATEHOOD

lo: i have seen written the equation of tender friendship

la: and have you ever seen written the equation of the villages of pleasing verses

lo: i have seen written the equation of the gallant letter

la: and have you ever seen written the equation of the land of tender

OBAMA OFFERS CONDOLENCES AS TOULOUSE STANDOFF CONTINUES

lo: i have seen the terms of the equation swirl both in fixed orbit and at random at every variable speed and on each plane of every world

la: have you seen the equation of the prophesy of the end of time

lo: the equation of the end of time mirrors the equation of war & peace

la: have you seen the equation of the streets

YOEL SILBER TAKING ON DANCE MUSIC ESTABLISHMENT IN TEL AVIV

lo: i have seen the complex equation which describes moses going through the city dressed as a beggar just for the fun of it just for play to see the people ascending as descending on the colored air collected from human breath made into art at peripatetic rituals

la: what's the equation for the relationship between the animal the vegetable and the mineral including the horse but exclusive of the super-orthodox rabbi of ecstasy

lo: i have seen written the equation of those lost in the quantum of indifference;;;; those calculating theories of advance and retreat on to and from amity

la: and do you believe what you see written?

US LAWMAKER RELEASES HOLD ON AID TO PALESTINIANS

lo: i believe that it's written. is that enough

la: in a world where the word enough is a term of inquisition

lo: for a time, i followed all the laws. each and every one of them. all the laws having to do with personal behavior; all the laws having to do with worship and ritual; all the laws concerning business transactions and social justice; all the laws having to do with the harmonies of nature. i only got more confused. i only got entangled in a net of laws until the net became the only law and it had to be destroyed it had to be broken asunder even if what lay ahead was not freedom or i didn't understand freedom

la: is the book itself the book of lies? the book of puzzles? the book of paranoid and beautiful letters?

IDF CHIEF OF STAFF GANTZ: NO COUNTRY CAN REMAIN ISOLATED FROM TERRORISM

lo: let's get back to some kind of reality, no? an equation of the peace of the middle east would do

la: reality? that's a funny word to play with. it's the only word that wants to be itself that wants to be what it names

lo: today i began a new life. i've constructed it from the pantomime of leather and flax. from oil. from the chance meeting of a him and a her. the foreordained correspondence of the mediterranean gods Gravitas & Levity

la: let's begin a discourse that will have no end throughout the generations: let's begin with a court of analysis into the guilt *and* the innocence of the words "new" and "life"

PLANNED NUMBER OF IRON DOMES CAN'T OFFER FULL PROTECTIONS

lo: while even birth isn't even the beginning

la: drop it. the only thing that might follow this dialogue between a *lo* and a *la* is a question whose answer belongs to someone else, neither to *lo* nor to *la*. whose answer is an equation beyond our mathematical beyond our astronomical abilities and belonging to the realm of the harmony of science and poetics

lo: and what about peace

la: and what about peace

ACT SAFELY ON NEW YEAR'S EVE SO YOU CAN ENJOY 2015

lo: and what about peace

la: and what about peace

MONITOR: NEARLY TWO THOUSAND PEOPLE EXECUTED BY ISIS IN SIX MONTHS

OCTOBER

Dream of light

        split by light

                abstract light

                        darkness   mistaken   for   light

memory of light

        the cry of light

                a bowl of light

                      light bent by gravity

                            weak light

first light

        light waves

                particles of light

                      light as a symbol of (love) (god) (truth)

last light

        the force of light

                light on water

                      light passing through water

           fear as light

                darkness as light

                      sexual light

artificial light

light as war

the time of light if light as the embodiment of time in the act of time's corroboration

light as food

an awakening from the dream of light

wine as light

the book of light

light also as peace, of course of course

the light of reason in light of

the light of the irrational

the poem as light but of a different order of linguatude

despair as light

the face of light

a faith in light as the last faith

the clarity of that light which illuminates human error

the light of human error

oedipus as light

freud as light

the light of pre-dawn

the light of dawn

the light of morning

the light of early afternoon

the light of high noon

the light of late afternoon

the light of dusk

the light of night

the light of pre-dawn

the light of aesthetic fury

the light at the end of the long long corridor

from light unto light

a desperate light

what is a soft light and when did it first come into being and why did it first come into being

the light that spins inside the nucleus of the atom the light of the atomic bomb

light as the word light

what if the light were not light what would it be

the light of the darkest flower of evil revealed

the light which tames the souls of all humankind

is the light which ensouls the rages of all humankind

the light that captures the earth

the light that takes the earth by lightstorm

the light that cannot be seen

the light that, among all the animals, is a powerful biological reality

the light that is as it is within the light that is not

the light by which we think whether it be of light or of darkness that we are thinking

the light of Van Gogh the light of Rembrandt the light of Giotto the light of Mark Rothko the light of Al Held all different fragments of light each one whole on its own

the light of my life the light in your eyes the light of your reason-affirming and your reason-annihilating laughter

the light of Whitman, the light of Rimbaud, the light of Williams the light of Messerli of Rebecca Goodman the light of Tod Thilleman the light of Dante the light of Pasquale Verdicchio the light of the formalist Shakespeare the light of the word the light of the words the light of all risks taken by writers leaping into and/or out of light the light of Calvino and Tutuola and Noam Mor and my dear goddess Woolf who yearned only to live on the earth as an equal to it.

the light which exists in the space which exists

the oxygen of light; the nitrogen of light
the photon of light; the ion of light; the electromagnetic radiation of light itself
visible to the naked human eye; the photosynthesis of light via the chemistry of
light into the light of organic life

& the scientists & the philosophers of light: Pythagoras Empedocles Epicurus
Euclid Ptolemy al-Khwārizmī al-Kindī Ibn al-Haytham Kitab al-Manazir Rog-
er Bacon all whether right or wrong for example whether light emanates from
objects or comes from the eye

the absence of light
                    the quest for light
                                   the light of the blind man/woman
                                           the light of health the light of disease
the light of the candle even just one candle even under the high noon sun on
          the desert floor

                                                  shared light
an explosion of light
              a blinding light
                    a false light
                              what happens to the sun's light as the earth turns
the light that infuses each one
              the light not in the white spaces but within the letters on each page
                                           the light which —
having abolished all darkness—had to be extinguished and by radical means
even violent means even perhaps in an act of self-eradication

the light which dropped a woman to her knees
                    I saw it

I was there I saw this with my own eyes

she lay prostrate before the light

I went to raise her up

but she had become light

and my hand passed through her

the light in the memory of your father

the light in the memory of your grandmother

the light in the eyes of michael furey that killed him

the light which replaces the darkness

which replaces the name which replaces the image that one has of oneself

whereby oneself we mean the universe the self of the universe

light to the light light: the lightness & the light ear—light—dwelt

upon until heard in each note of Eric Satie the light in the capricious and mur-

derous and the sweetest touch of Beethoven in the constructed liberty of Bach

in the dramaterror of Igor Stravinsky in the meandering lightseeking riff of Mr

John Coltrane the light in the very idea of music from the very beginning of

time not even the beginning of humankind but the literal the beginning of time

that music which is the light of time which itself goes neither backwards nor

forwards in its composition

I knew the woman who had fallen to her

knees and then to prostration she had come from my village—as a child—I had

watched her: in fascination; from a guarded distance—a distance guarded by

what: by dread? by desire?

the light in

depression; the light in anxiety.

the light which goes on which has no end no

purpose the light which replaces prayer with silence even though light itself

cannot carry silence into its form or emit silence from its form they—all those from that village of my childhood—had for so long expected to see a certain light manifest waiting to see it that when it appeared on the shores of the great lake they denied it at first they ran from it they accused it of deviltry they tried to kill it but in the end they absorbed it as it became a part of them so unrecognizable so disfamiliar that they never again knew who they were while some of them found it funny just funny as hell or paradise

the light of the authority of light the light at the heart of the joke of nature where our continuous laughter abides as a full spectrum of color

the light of history as it evolves renaming the pursuit of happiness the pursuit of power the pursuit of justice the quest for survival the march of the progress of mankind the light of socialism of capitalism of communism pure and simple and of those movements in which we find no light no light at all but then the light of the imp of the perverse revealed in our continuous laughter our own confessions of freedom

the light of solitude which desires solitude—and yearns for the communion of solitude and yearns for the light of companionship—which desires companionship and yearns for the light of the communion of companionship

the light of the dream only dreamt of

the light in the acts of communion

the light in waiting

the light in the yard the light in the house the light in the room the light on the sides of the buildings the light in sound the light in friction the light in motion

the light in enmity

the light in discovery

the light which the scriptures tell us goes from generation to generation and which it calls an eternal light while we smile across time at the authors of those scriptures who still believed in the myths they so delighted even lived in

A DIALOGUE AT THE FAR END OF THE WORLD

No. My children do not come to see me. I have no children. I was a victim...a subject of Mengele. He took away from me my ability to give birth.

You...?

Yes. He performed his experiments on me.

And you...?

Yes. Me.

And so you have no....?

Listen to me. Yes, I was a victim of Mengele. And just now...in my long life...I am 92 years old now...just recently...I have seen I have known I have begun to live who I truly am. Who I am which is the not-Mengele and not even the not-Mengele. Further. Farther. Can you possibly understand my triumph?

I...I don't know.

You will.

I will?

Yes. Because I choose you to. You are young.

Not so young.

But you will come to understand. I will it and so will it be.

My mother....

She....?

Yes. Your friend....

No. My acquaintance. Your mother is trivial. You are not trivial.

You befriended my mother to get to me?

I didn't know about you. She didn't even talk about you. Now you come here and I meet you in this garden and it's the first I've heard of you.

But you found me.

I chose you. I didn't invent you. I chose you. Or...no. You found me.

Why would I?

Who knows why?

I thought you needed me.

I do. I need just one person on this Earth to know my triumph.

OK. I will be that person – for you. But why do I need you?

Because you need to know what's possible in this life. And you need to know the price one might have to pay to achieve it.

I do?

Yes. You do.

IN LOVE

in love

      there was

             a sacrifice

     to be taken

            lightly

     that is

            to be given

                    and to be self-

                    given

      - a gift -

meant

        if at all

to lead

        to some

        knowledge

     to wisdom

                   of some kind never quite

        imagined

                     feared

                     even as

                     as desired

                     even as

as hungered for

an opening

in a field

of openings

continuum

breastbone and breathplate

ii.

in crimea

now

we are at the diplomacy

of novels & of fictions we are

at the forefront

of the glory

of home so then & here we are &
here are we at jerusalem the new bloomusalem xtianjewianmuslumian jerusalem

city of cities

town of towns

village/villagers

pillages

iii

the wound is empty

is the wound empty?

iv

in the morning

after the zodiacal light

the voices awaken

        in the cribroom

    the baby lying faceup on the plane

    eyeswide watches stars as herds

of elephants trumble past

        raising the duststorms of distant

    memories billions of years hence

        that pass through the eye

    of a brain

    awakening

      synapses

       of speech

v

paul celan at the window

    walt whitman in the hospitals of washington d.c.

the baseball season opens with the pitcher throws the batter swings a homerun over the left-field fence dives into home plate for the sheer drama for the crowdsucking joy of it the crowd leaves the stadium the silence prevails in the rosy-fingered dusk dogs and cats they take to the field the grass grows to the height of wheat the owners sell it for a dollar a bushel

mrs. lebyensnikov and mrs. potemkin and mrs. kropotkin gather around the television to witness fire of putin pour from his mouth into their livingroom where the table hosts them on borschts on beefs on mayonnaise where they raise over it all the flag of sorrows where they weep so heartfeltfully for the grandchildren of mrs. lebyensnikov and mrs kropotkin who will not die in the wars to will come no they have moved on to queens new york carrying the homeland in their hearts but the granddaughter of mrs. potemkin will die tomorrow caught in the cross-fire of sevestapol her body languishing in the street for 11 hours until two passing children carry it off to bury it with honors

franz kafka will write in a letter to the ny times: i am weary of guilt and rage i see myself filled with light with joy i see all my people led by maimonades dance in the streets of kafkusalem i will join the dodgers in los angeles i will be the baseball soaring over the sea

12:12 p.m. After

        I wrote

            that letter

        in those letters in those

              words

to the n.y. times

        i stumbled upon these

    words: he who is lost

              will not be found he

     who is urgent

            will remain unnamed he

   who communes with the silence

               will find silence

     in his pockets he

           can outwait himself

  from his other precarious pocket

          he pulls out a clown

    holding a sign that says:

         silence

         is action

INTERSGERS

in the interplay

    between human beings

        and impersonal forces

            comes the windstorm.

                in the dynamic

    between the classic

        and the romantic

            comes the voice

              of the economies

                of our daily bread.

in the discourse

    between the altar

        and the workshop

            comes the symbol

              comes the instinct the flair

      the strokes

      of un/analy/sable genius

in the dance

    between the hero

        and the villain

        comes the self

            born   of the union

of beauty

　　　and pain

in the communion

　　　of freedom

　　　and oblivion

　　　　　comes clarity

　　　carried by an actor

　　　raised by her

　　　on a tray

　　　as　　perpetually　　she

　　　crosses

　　　　　the horizon

in the action

in the action

　　　of the horse

　　　and the horseman

　　　　　　comes the virtuosity

　　　　　　　　of the ir-

　　　　　　　reversible comes

　　　and arises

　　　the singular voice

　　　plural

AN DISAMBIGUITY

the answer to the railroad is the disambiguity of sex and the realization of time is the placement of the answers in a row the earth has no identity but it does have relativity it has relatives each atom has no identity but it does have specificity it has never existed until the moment of its liberation from the constraints of nothingness let's not get too abstract here let's tell the truth as in the story of the man who went out into the desert to weep alone at the loss he could not name he became a lizard he became a white moon he became the disambiguity of sand he became the enemy he became the comrade the companion he did not become the light the light is the light. but we were telling a story we had story in mind. when the man arrived at the sunshine he took off his dream. when he arrived at the cornerstone he took off memory. when he arrived at the air he remembered who he might become and what were his obligations to form the realities of sight and the waves of change. he stood up to build a house made of wheat made of motion made of molten sound. she took an ax to hew animal from stone. she wrote on the lintel: the will to change is the action of being is the constancy of ebullience is the rage for communion is the community of desire. she opened the door. she crossed the beginning. she was in the other world. the one they had drawn with crayons. a train passed by. he jumped down from it. he was sober. he was whole and intact. he was a man and a woman. he was the bark of a tree. he was wheat.

THE LAST DELUSION

Nothing is disallowed but everything turns into someone else

The sum total of all knowledge is a glass of water on a table in sunlight

The things of the world—be they brown black blue yellow green white orange magenta—belong to our eyesight where they remain unnamed

Hope is not for life eternal and everlasting but for energy which is that which supersedes life eternal and life everlasting

The difference between revenge and success is a mirror on a table in sunlight

Trouble in the family can be resolved only in a dance of the rages of memory performed by the witches who walk off into a cloud to emerge where we cannot see them doing what we know not what

I want more tomatoes

I want more apples

I want more oranges

I want figs

I want pomegranates

I want

     grapes

In the marketplace a man sits with bowls of spices before him when out of his opening chest pours forth a cornucopia when I approach him his boy says to me this is the depths of a summer you have never seen anything like it before it contains the depths of winter which you cannot see now no need to see when I pull from my pocket coins pour forth when I turn around the newly painted letters on the ancient wall read we refuse to be enemies the elderly man a sculptor stands smiling waving his hat in the air singing a song of freedom singing I am free from myself we are free from each other

The taste of food like the history of time lingers on the tongue

When walking in the city or the fields it is easier to imagine the night during the day than to imagine the day during an eclipse of the trees easier to imagine the absence of zero than it is to remember the name of the God you grew up with as a child and easier to imagine wealth among the beggars than to retrieve water from the heart of a deck of playing cards dealt by the hand of the rich or is it easier to steal the deuce of diamonds from the eye of a storm or to arrange the molecules taken from a radiation cloud into the sphere of a dandelion into the curvature of the shape of one life expanding since the big bang

By the waters of downtown we drank cool draughts of insight of courage we drank directly from the night

& what can it mean to write without words what can it mean to swim around the globe what can it mean to energize leaps of change in evolution what can it mean to walk into the aboriginal cave all the way to the end to touch the wall to open the award of speech

The Ourgos and the Demiourgos, walking down the Street, Sand, side by side. They become One then they become human. At a saltable by the seaside human takes the seasalt plants it grows it into waterharest feeds the horse is something new

the world is new

again the horse divides the human divides the Ourgos and the Demiourgos split apart kiss each other goodbye for now one into the temple of marble and glass the other into the sanctuary of love and destitution the humans in the open field ready to answer the question that will come their way to and unto each other one another   with her fore/finger

          the mother   traces   the distinct   features   in the face
of the father's son

The energy of being the red light afloat in the skyfog at dawn. again.

The double helix at memory reinforces the repetition of chaos formed into the atomic order of the day rising from sleep or disaster to begin the day that day a scientist will discover what she will call the error of the universe to begin her search for a correction in the release of energy embodied in politics or war in psyche or art

There is a barrier falling from eternity into the lap of the golden child voices come from everywhere some of them green some yellow some gleam in the distance some dance around the nightmare honed perfected relevant to a civilization as a whole beware. there is a hole in the second hand of the clock fall through see what's there on the inside see what feels like damp and solid earth take it into the mouth digest it feed the cells of the living molecules of hunger whose thirst for a moment's beatitude reveals the structure of the wind in which to see across into the sleep of the other

We bring the passionate parties into the room together we let them slug it out we know we will find them together in an embrace of love or death here is where a man damned his enemy to hell his entire wish was fulfilled here is the collection of ancient musical instruments which he picks up one by one by one to sound the reverberations of a tender joy as the wounded lover wakens

all night in the dark she reads the illuminated manuscripts until she says the word sleep then the crows fly away

something happens in the moment changes history a bullet or an act of listening for us who think ourselves on the verge of something who have always been in the midst of it only the angel of the real can ride from wave to wave only that angel tell us what matter is what matters is what can suck out the heart what save it. again.

fury will release the objects of the world from stasis into the atomic whirlwind of formchange

Openness is all openness is all openness is all. . . . .

An imaginary skyline against an actual sky. Take away the sky. Replace the sky. Take away the skyline.

In the park the preacher proclaims that "there is no shade in Paradise for there the Glory of God and the Radiance of Eternity is comfortable and they are a balm and an unction to every pain of man and beast." In the shadow of the olive tree, where we stand, laying your arm around my shoulder, you say to me, "where has my youth gone?" Nuzzling in to your arm I sweep a gesture around the park, saying, "Look. Everywhere." You say, "My friend, even after the war, you are an optimist." "Or a child," I say. "Or a child," he says, "full of delusions." "Or a man," I say. "Or a man," he repeats me, "absent of delusions." "Absent," he follows me, "of delusions," asking me "does that mean empty or full?"

The architecture of mind moves toward or away from or both at once.

The air breathes the water hydrates the soil mulches bromine iodine nitrogen god does not exist because to exist means to be known and we can't even in the definitions of the believers we cannot know god god is the unknown and the unknown does not exist because to exist means to be known there are destructive impulses in the hearts of humankind and we must come to know them there are creative impulses in the hearts of humankind and we must come to return them to whom they belong

EXISTS

the world
        exists
as it   is

close
        your eyes
look
at the world

open
        your eyes
the world exists
as it will be

       for tyler hardy

BLANK PAGE

there is movement in the shadows
cast by light and objects
there is no such question as what
will i write for the blank page
is already written the bells
and the crows make no sense
make only nonsense the nonsense
we listened for
as we followed the railroad tracks
heaving, curving into straightaways
the grammatical structure
of the landscape unfolding
there
the music of silence is not
a sentimental idea it is the root
of all water it is the core
of earthquakes it is the marketplace
of fair exchange in the midst
of the urge for double dealing
listen! we are the species
who can answer the questions that memory
poses we
are the ones who re/invent
language each day
to speak in communication
with the buildings to rush
through the blood of the polis to negotiate
the sexual maze to arrive

at the theater on time
to bear witness to the surd
to watch
the animals
in their hunting rituals
to speak out
here i am and to fall
back into
an armchair
of who am i
of ambiguous—no—of chaotic—no—of sinister—no of complex—no—
of insistent—no of transitory—no of ridiculous—no of heartfelt—no—of
wise—no—of disturbing—no—of self-sustaining—no—of the heavening
of hellling—no of the helling of heavening—no of the peace that passeth
understanding—no—of the no—no of the—yes of the absolutely no of the
necessary—no of the tranquil—no—of the blood-curdling—no of the rap-
turous—no of the ordinary of the merely and the simply daily—no of the
enigmatic entry into energy—no of the pathos of—no of the denial—no of
the mutinous—no of the spacious—no of the imprisoned—no—of the aque-
ous—no of the malfunctioning—no of the blissful—no of the sorrowful—no
of the silent smiling of the smile of the smiling

such movement write
cast question crows
sense shadows nonsense written light
page what which i will
nonsense
objects by blank there
there bells make make
are is already the and for is
for the only the
the the
listened
we

ANCIENT CITY OF THE ANCIENT WORLD

.... the visible walls of the invisible structure
downfall under the weight of
                    centuries a simple
                    an engineering inevitability

In the redishbrown day all words
          collide beyond the speed of light
          in indelible indestructions

                    a man and two women
                    in formal dress
                    cross the piazza

                              in the light
          of the noonésday
          sun
          a light impossible to swallow without
                              becoming
                              oneself
                              pure light

          though the eyes pulsate
          the memory stores
          its hosts of good & evil
to draw upon
                    for the orchestration
                    of spontaneous

                    musicians
swaying in the rhythm
            in polyrhythms   chaosrhythms

reverberates into the
stone walls of the invisible
structure

            to instigate their release

into silencepresence to say
the indefensible beauty
the sign of generations

the red shoes
of the innocencecriminal
escaping detection

                i cried out
                hosound
                hosound

the ordinary something
of the everyday crossroads

the man meets the boy
in the mutual swallowing
of the other

                based on a theme
on a progression
of tonalities

                        on a palette splintered
                        by a prism
held up in front of
the **Big Eye** to absorb

BECAUSE OF JOSEPH PERLOFF & RENE CREVEL

that there is no distance between the thing and the knowing of the thing means that we are not as alone as we have come to believe ourselves to be—unless, perversely, in anger or guilt or rage or fear—we withdraw within ourselves to that place we alone create—where we alone abide—but why would we do that —already—each of us—remembering the traumas of birth. while we cannot grasp this absence of distance with our understanding—we might say that it exists outside of time and space—and that to ask whether it precedes us or not displays our ignorance of the facts. that we cannot name this absence of distance is not a failure of language nor is it a triumph of silence wherein there is no distance between language and silence. language is a feast made of the digits of silence silence is a feast made of the alphabets of babylon. we do not need language to name it nor do we need extraordinary gestures of tenderness or violence to approach it. all we need is art or science or mathematics. all we need is to click our heels. all we need is to listen to the neurons of the heartbrain predicting the future. all we need to do is to find the curved line of spacetime and to lay ourselves along it.

BECAUSE OF MARY CORSE

the color white is white as the color white as the word is the color
word as the brain is the color speed as the now is the color of
motion as the kiss is as kisses as the color kiss as the color of absence
is the absence is the color of the color of absence is the color of
the core of the planet earth is the earth of the color seeing & the
color of energy is the same as the color green is as green as the
color green but it is not the color green which is as yellow as the
color word which is as word as the word is or the word as or the
word self or the word enigmawhite or the word blindwhite or the
which word which is as chair as the word chair is chair but which
is not the chair but the word chair which the infant takes into its
mouth to suck on as if it were the word god or the word born or
the word of a parentage of White and White both of whom born
of the parentage White and Word both of whom born of the
parentage Word and White none of it at all incestuous but of
the timeworld where all words are the same word yet meaning
is conveyed clearly as clearly is absolutely as is absolutely white

JOURNEY TO LOVE

the delusions appear across the horizon & beyond the bobo trees that hang
sweetly from the autumn. the names of all the species parade dressed in the
most elaborate costumes—so festive. a drum roll. a curtain rising. a bright
white light no one can see. a circusmaster. the white horse. two wrestlers. a
young man delivers a speech full of sound fully furious. sixteen puppets dance
to the tune of a wind that blows through the opening chapter. by the end of
the book everyone is weeping although whether in sorrow or in joy none of
them know. the sweeper comes through with her ancient broom to sweep away
the ancient papers of the last of the ancien régime. the stars are aligned for
fortuitous announcements forthcoming from the arts academy. dancers are
followed by poets. followed by the artist of thinking. followed by the artist of
inclinations / impulses / emotions. followed by the artist of all white space.

followed by the artist of light. followed
by the artist of love. ah, here he comes. fresh forth from the womb of rivers.
fresh from the teeth of the lion. fresh from the fury of the wastelands far to the
depths of the stage. followed by the artist of illusions. followed by the sea. followed by the whole sea.

LIME

The reflection
      of the freshly picked
                lime
        in the glass
tabletop
      at morning
           reifies
     the release
        of the prisoner
   after twenty-two years
     six months
         four days
              five hours
        and sixteen minutes
        of imprisonment
   by error
            into freedom

EROS

Life began long ago it never stops
that beginning
the purchase exchange
of your groceries
is a form of this beginning
the glass door
sliding
on its hinges
is a form
of this beginning death
is a form
of this beginning
to imagine
a world
absent of thought
altogether
is to encounter
this beginning
which began
so long ago it is
a long ago
yet to come
even as
it is coming
just now

Life
began long ago
long
before its beginning
life began long ago
long before
the telescope long
before carbon long
before hydrogen long long
before oxygen
long before time
or the curvature of space
life begins
it keeps to begin
inside

of a small nodule
inside the brain
of humankind
even as
life began
as is material & life
begins long before
the radical forgetting
of mankind

ii

Life begins and begins
without our knowing it
while we wash
the dishes while we are confused
about identity and
history while we call out

for the return of what might have been lost
along a way along a long long way

iii

Life began
in the way of course
where there is no such thing
as beginning
and this is the invention
of the joke
upon which we rely
to heal the scar
of beginnings to open
the distances
of an inhabitation

iv

That life began
does not predict
any ending
This
is a beginning
which engenders beginning
This
is the fornication
which does not arise
or cease
and which has no knowledge
of desire

WHITE[10]

No despair is equal to the color white. But what is despair?

What is white?

No. I asked you: what is despair?

If you left me I'd fall into a terrible despair.

Why?

Without you......I don't know. I don't know why. It frightens me come
   to think of it.

So love keeps us from despair?

Why not?

Because I want to go bare naked in the world.

You think love just masks despair? Does it?

You said it. You said that if I left you you'd despair.

Look. What's more true? Is love less true less authentic less real than
   despair?

Can we be together and you'd still feel despair?

Sure. Sometimes I'm sure. But not the same.

Love assuaging despair?

Or heightening it....

Because? No escape?

No escape.

I reached for the glass of wine on the night table. She had to move her arm, roll off my chest. I had to sit up to sip the wine. She sits up. I hold the glass for her to her lips.

Are you sleepy? she asks me.

Are you?

Yes. But more than sleepy.

How more?

I want to turn over. I want you to put your arm around me. I want to close my eyes. I want—in the darkness of my vision in my still my sweet drunkenness in my post-coital malaise to indulge in the beauties of despair and love.

As they are a comfort to you?

Yes. A balm to my vivid mind.

Then roll over.

I put my arm around her.

Are your eyes closed?

Yes.

And what do you see? What do you feel?

I'm alone, Harry. I'm terribly awfully alone. It's painful. I could cry.

That's not despair is it?

No, darling, it's not. Or it is. I don't know. Do you love me?

Completely.

Good night.

Good night.

Harry?

Yes?

It's passed now.

The despair?

I feel so light now. Heavenly light.

—

It's joy, Harry. I feel real joy. I do.

I love your joy.

And do you love my despair?

—

Yes.

—

—

But I hate my own.

I don't Harry I don't. Rare that it is.

I drew her closer to me, and she came.

Have we come through? she asked me.

Yes, I said, we have come through.

We slept. In the morning, we begin again. The cat follows me into the kitchen. I make coffee. She still sleeps. I dress for work. I take coffee for her into the bedroom but she still sleeps. No need to wake her. Let her sleep.

As I drink my coffee—as alone as I'll ever be—the gardener mows the lawn next door. That noise. My solitude. And. And because and is an and. Is not an end but an and. And I sit here writing this—in my solitude—on paper—with pen—as the paper opens a great hole—onto—on to and....and I am writing through that hole on wind. Each word I write carries away the wind each wind I write—.... I write *despair*—the wind carries it away. I write *joy*—the wind carries it away. I am the wind writing on wind. Each word is the word wind. Until—my amazing daughter—not yet born—only a desire—sits on my lap her hand into the paperswind writing her name on that wind her name is amazingdaughter. We go further we go further. There is no return. There is always returning. I go upstairs. I walk into the windroom your hair blown winderly I kiss you you only stir I straighten my tie I leave for work I keep going there is no return there is no Harry there is Harry returning to where he never left from. I have solved the case. The lawnmower is quiet. I go looking for our love. It is there in everyroom. It is in each apology and apologia. I lie down with you. Returning. Into the wind. Who gave me this body gave you this body. Is this my body or is this your body? Am I the wind or are you the wind? I say wake up but you are already wakened. You are writing these words this memoir because only you remember the truth. All I remember are advertisements for carnal spirituality. I close my eyes. In the wind that blows through the darkness I see you—awakened—watch me sleep—guard my newly-formed soul—until you get up you walk away I am an amazing daughter who knows that you that a you that every you that each you all yous will return and return.

The door opens. It is night. Yet light breaches the horizon. While I want it to stay night so that I might go out walking in it feeling it against my face my skin the light keeps rising. Then it is daylight and I am walking in daylight—feeling it against my skin. I rub it into my eyes.

SUBWAY

in the flowering of the subway station the straight lines cross through dimension meet the delineated curvatures of space at where the man meets the woman they argue at first but then they're ok there's not enough money for the rent the faceless man signs the fulfillment of the speed of the railway cars the workers lay new track for a new train going to the city center where the action is the laying of the track itself is action the workers men and women sweat in the darkness of the tunnel guided by the indivisible soundwaves shouting out illuminating phrases in the flowering of the fields the man lies down beside the woman they stare at the sky they disappear along the straight lines that cross through dimension to meet the delineated curvature of time toward the seedgrass

AN END OF VIOLENCE[2]

getting on the elevator at its lowest level, you push the button for the first floor.
a thin man, holding a photograph, makes sweeping motions with a small, inci-
sive, sharp sharp knife over the photograph of a woman. the elevator ascends.
turning toward you, the man threatens you with the knife. at your arms. at your
torso. at your daze. you are in a daze. in a stupor. in a lostness of vivid contem-
plation. just as the elevator comes to the thin man's stop: the 184th floor—you
awaken. the doors open onto the sky. you push the man out. leaning over just
slightly, holding on to nothing, you look down. he falls endlessly. as the elevator
descends—on the way down—fear invades you, rises through you. you allow it
you give it access you grant it trespass. you don't know where it comes from. you
reach your destination. the first floor. the doors open. onto the sky. gazing, the
blue expanse, you hold the doors open for some time. then you step out, walking
on the sky out of the skybuilding onto the sidewalk where the crowds pass where
a saxophonist plays for change. you throw a penny into his saxophone case. he
plays louder. he plays cooler. he plays with more verve he enters abandon. leaning over, the saxaphonist takes up the penny, hands it back to you. you take it.
put it in your pocket. there is nothing special about it. it is an ordinary penny.
but, burning a hole in your pocket it falls to the ground and you walk on you
walk on you walk on. you pass a newsstand with a photograph hanging up for
sale—it's the woman in the photograph in the elevator. taking it down, you turn,
but the owner has you by the arm. "and who are you!" "that's me," you gesture
towards the photo. "i'm the woman in the photograph." "sorry," the owner says,
"i didn't see it at first." he lets you go. you walk on. at the tramstop, a woman
holds a child in her arms. the child rests his head on the mother's shoulder. you

do not recognize the mother. you recognize the child, but you don't know where from.

you step through the open window. it is the photograph of the woman.

WHIRL

the becoming of the anthracite the commingling of the elements the wholeness of the earth that reveals its eminence in repetitions of its fame in returning to the day of sand the eve of portentous nuances

the animal has not yet fully entered his being being numerous being alliterative of each other each letter swallows the text each thought that encumbers the nuance of time oh alleluah all my music is sung all my people are known

OF MEMORY

the end
of memory
is time
the end of
memory
is the
opening
of the hour
the end of
memory is
the transition
seamless from
world to world
the end of
memory is the
beginning of the
beautiful sleep

HOW TO ENTER

the gateway to the philosophy of time is opened by the golden key of cups

the gateway to the science of time is opened by the number 6

the gateway to the aesthetics of time is open always opening

ASTRONOMY

the minute

        wearing a mask

    walks away

       from the history of time

the sky's light is again a sexual enigma
      bound up
      in the shoulders of memory's end

the same earth created at what we call our beginning

       is the site of intimate festivals
       is the intimacy of constant change
       is the constants of food and fire

          in our universe
          light
          is escaping
          from a black hole
          that will be
          discovered
          by an astronomer priest
          from the vatican
          observatory
          in ghana

we are
light
escaping

from a black hole

our name is one plus one
the exact formula
of our light
will be discovered

TOUCH

The only thing that has no form is consciousness.

The only thing that has form are these words.

The form whose form changes constantly millisecond by millisecond is consciousness.

The only thing that ever loses form entirely are these words.

If it has no totality of presence in it if it has no access to absence in it
it is neither form nor formless nor does it partake
of the universe in its origin as desire

BECAUSE OF PAUL ELUARD

which is more in
                    complete   the day
                                              or the

               night

which is more incom /
                    plete   the sun
                                        or the moon

which
          is more incomplete   the man in the red hat
                                              or the woman at the beach

which is more incomplete

                    the present
                              or the past

which is more incomplete   the president of Uruguay
                                        or the ballet dancer

which is more incomplete   the boat
                                              or the airplane

which is more incomplete   the adolescent
                                              or the infant

which is more in com plete   the news
                              paper

or the poem/book

which

       is more incomplete   the barren tundra

                           or the City of Siam

which is more incomplete   history

                        or science mathematics

                               or psychology

which is more incomplete   the doctor

                        or the patient

which is more incomplete

                    monday

                          or now

      even if now is also

                    monday

which is more incomplete   love

                  or love

which is more incomplete   the joy

                  or the fear

which is more incomplete   the painting

                        or the painter

which is more incomplete   the student

                            or the teacher

which is more incomplete   the neurosis

                        or the psychosis

which is more incomplete   the finite

                  or the timeless

which is more incomplete   world war I

                                 or world war II

                                      the korean

                                          war

                                                or the war in vietnam

which is more in//complete   catholicism

                                    or buddhism

which is more in//complete   women's liberation

                                      or the civil rights movement

which is more incomplete   beethoven's fifth symphony

                              or the psalm 151 of peter eötvos

which is more incomplete   psalm 151

                                    or the new york times

which is more incomplete   humans

                                  or alphabets

which is more incomplete   israel

                            or palestine

which is more incomplete thought or being
which is more complete

which is more incomplete   the railroad
                   or the aniseed growing where it doesn't belong in Africa
which is more incomplete   the sound

                              or the aftersound

which is more incomplete   the reading

                              or the image

which is more incomplete   history

or geology

which is more incomplete   self

or love

or the self that is love

or the love that is self

which is more incomplete   the violence of nations

or the peace of nations

which is more incomplete   the communion within families

or the conflict within families

which is more incomplete   greek literature

or hebrew literature

greek myth

or hebrew myth

or the myth of modernity

or the myth of science which is

more incomplete

which is more incomplete   the home

or the wandering

which is more incomplete   the circle

or the broken circle

which is more incomplete

the city house

or the country house

the suburbs

or the farm

the mountains

or the sea

which is more incomplete   the supermarket

or the drugstore

which is more incomplete   the song
                                        or the dance which

is more incomplete   the dancer
                                        or the dance

which is more incomplete   the fire
                                        or the fire that burns the fire

which is more incomplete   the political prisoner entering prison
                                        or the political prisoner exiting prison

which is more incomplete   the dove
                                        or the bread

which is more incomplete   the secret
                                        or the destruction of the hour

which is more weightless
                    the discovery of psyche
                                        or the discovery of the knife & the
fork

which is more incomplete
                    faces remembered
                                        or faces forgotten

which is more incomplete   the lake
                                        or the sea
                                        the stream
                                                    or the fountain

which is more incomplete   asleep
                                        or awake

which is more incomplete
                    breaking up with your girlfriend

                                        or starting up with a new girlfriend

which is more incomplete   breakfast
                                                or dinner

which is more incomplete   time
                                        or the sun

which is more incomplete   k-mart
                                                or t-mobile

which is more incomplete   the parallelogram
                                or the square root of the speed of the tumbleweed

which is more incomplete   the known
                                                or the unknown

which is more incomplete

                                the saint
                                                        or the common man

which is more incomplete   the finite
                                        or the gyroscope
                                                the infinite
                                                        or the habitude
which is more incomplete
                                the liberation of time
                                                or the engines of industry
which is more incomplete   the woman raking the leaves
                                        or the lawn and the sidewalk after
                                                the woman raking the leaves

which is more incomplete   the joy of the incomplete
                                        or the awe of the incomplete

which is more incomplete   the father
                                                or the son

which is more incomplete   the never

                                                      or the nowhere

which is more incomplete   the orgasm

                                           or the post-orgasm

which is more incomplete   love

                                             or the need for love

which is more incomplete   the hunter

                                                   or the hunted

& which is more incomplete   the music

                                                      or the song

& which

          more

                    incomplete

                    the poet

                    or the poem

which is more incomplete   the writing

                                             /or the written

& which
is more incomplete
the saxophone
or the piano
                    the violin

                              or the violin

                                        or the violin

                                                  or the violin

                              or the violin

MAN & NATURE

when you speak the ocean speaks
in fact all of the seas speak

this is so patently false and stupid and ridiculous
that it's obvious

and it goes without saying that it is true that while
oceans of water may not appear to pour forth from your mouth
even so when you speak and so forth

the streets all criss-cross the city in patterns
of birth

THE IDEA OF POETRY AS WITNESSED

Where the idea is love the resolution is its opening. Where the idea is the love of things as they are at a given moment of time the invocation is the solid sentence that approaches meaning. Where the idea is the liberation of idea from the tyranny of hysterias against it the idea illuminates its maturity. The wind blows all the branches of the olive tree around and around. The gardener with his earphones and his mower races across the lawn across and across. Time is money. The reader scans the words and the lines on the page to absorb the ideashapes of the letters shaped by the arrogance of the flippancy of the idea of creation. Those who can read it will read it. Otherwise goes home. Where the idea is the odor of fresh cut grass after the noise of the grasscutter as the grasscutter crosses the grasslawn the idea of the fleeting impermanence of the senses slows down his pace & he hears the tv next door broadcasting the ball game. Where the idea is the impermanence of the senses the senses win because they're real. Where is the idea that drives the poem is it in the rhythm is it in the time or in the timelessness of reading is it in resolution as opening

EXIST: AN OPERA FOR AN UNDETERMINATED NUMBER OF VOICES

i exist. unequivocally, i exist. while I always suspected this, i've confirmed it. how? the unraveling of that how remains to be the core of this existence I have discovered. one sage has written that god is that entity to whom we can attribute no positive traits: god is not infinite, not just, not kind, not compassionate, not indifferent. this is the existence i've discovered. this existence has nothing to do with whether i am kind or cruel, passionate or banal, lost or found. that's the most stunning quality of it. that it has no qualities. is that frightening? is it alienating? is it reassuring? is it anything at all? or is it everything at all? and if i exist, does the world exist? and if the world exists, does god exist? when did i discover this? i sat at a table dining with others. the conversation went on around me. was i speaking when i discovered this? was i silent? it was not i who discovered this, it was i who discovered this. no one else saw that discovery no one felt it or heard it no one knew or knows anything about it because i can't tell anyone about it because the i who would tell anyone is not the i who knows about it so it would be secondhand news what the lawyers call hearsay. hearsay. think about it. hearsay. such an interesting word. hearsay. here's what they were saying at that table.

I spent a hundred and fifty dollars on it but i got every penny's worth.

Uhm, I saw it for ninety-nine ninety-five.

No! Where?

That's right. Nowhere.

Laughter.

Have you seen the show on nowhere at the museum downtown?

How can a show about nowhere be downtown?

Laughter.

More wine?

Thank you.

No, thank you.

Because downtown is nowhere.

Clever, but, meaning....?

Oh, yes I can. Meaning that it's all huge skyscraping buildings with offices where no one exists.

Does anyone exist anywhere? Or do we all exist nowhere?

Enough sophistry!

Never enough sophistry!

Words! Words!

Did you really see it for ninety-nine ninety-five?

Well, I just told you that to get a rise out of you.

To make me feel foolish.

I wouldn't do that. Just having fun.

Not fun. It's not fun.

Don't be so sensitive.

A ritual came our way.

How things have changed by remaining the same!

I have no ideas to convey, but other kinds of things.

Life isn't worth it. It isn't even worth it.

Oh yes it is. It certainly is.

Who are you? And how do you know anything?

I've been there.

Where?

Where life isn't worth it.

I don't think so.

And there we were on the battle field at Plenum. We looked up and we looked out to see the enemy coming at us full hurtle full speed full fury.

And what did you do?

We held our ground. We took our positions. We trembled and we shook and we held our positions.

And....?

And we watched.

And....?

And they disappeared! The enemy. They dis-a-p-peared. It was the damndest damn thing that any of us had ever seen in all our born days combined. We didn't get to kill a one of them.

Or they you.

The body is the house of the Lord.

The house of the bored?

No, not the bored, you idiot, the house of the Lord.

Pray, then?

Yes, we better.

For what? Pray for what?

For rain, for I sense a rain coming.

Lovely.

Yes. Who doesn't love the rain when you're indoors watching out the window hearing the rain on the windows on the roof the rain and the wind together a Duet in E Major for rain and wind

Sipping a scotch.

Not I. I hate the rain wherever whenever. I love only the sunshine. I'm a sunworshiper.

You're a pagan then!

OK. A pagan I'll be, and all you Jews and all you Christians and all you Buddhists and all you Muslims and all you Jain and all you witches you're all pagans in fancy churches.

i exist. unequivocally, i exist. while I always suspected this, i've confirmed it. how? the unraveling of that how remains to be the core of this existence I have discovered. one sage has written that god is that entity to whom we can attribute no positive traits: god is not infinite, not just, not kind, not compassionate, not indifferent. this is the existence i've discovered. this existence has nothing to do with whether i am kind or cruel, passionate or banal, lost or found. that's the most stunning quality of it. that it has no qualities. is that frightening? is it alienating? is it reassuring? is it anything at all? or is it everything at all? and if i exist, does the world exist? and if the world exists, does god exist? when did i discover this? i sat at a table dining with others. the conversation went on around me. was i speaking when i discovered this? was i silent? it was not i who discovered this, it was i who discovered this. no one else saw that discovery no one felt it or heard it no one knew or knows anything about it because i can't tell anyone about it because the i who would tell anyone is not the i who knows about it so it would be secondhand news what the lawyers call hearsay. hearsay. think about it. hearsay. such an interesting word. hearsay. here's what they were saying at that table.

And then, when they liberated that prison they found my husband wandering in rags through rubble. They brought him here. They knocked on my door. They said they had found him. They said I should come to claim him like some bag of clothes or something. I went to find him at their office but he couldn't speak. For six years he couldn't speak. Do you know what that's like, living with that?

And now?

And now he says things I love to hear—beautiful things beautifully said—but things I can't understand.

Have you voted?

Yes.

For whom, may I ask?

I don't remember. It was one or the other.

What does he talk about?

He talks about everything, but especially art. He's come to love art so much.

What kind of art?

All kinds. Ancient Greek sculpture. Impressionists. Modern, all those schools, Post-Modern. Color Field. Renaissance. Flemish. All of it. He devours it.

even if i'm dreaming, i exist, the dream of my existence exists even though it's not this dream that is my existence.

Why when my uncle was dying last week he murmured to me almost in a daze a dream not a delirium but a trance he said that even though he knew he was dying he felt he was being born that he was slipping in to life yes he said I'll tell you exactly though I'm a little embarrassed that he felt he was slipping in to the womb from which he was to be born isn't that just incredible

Even among all my Newport Rhode Island wispiest waspiest friends you know anti-semitism they don't accept that anymore.

Well for a while now it's not fashionable now but it will be again.

No no you must see it the structure of society is changing has changed.

That's good. You must be right. Fashions change and they don't come back do they?

Ach, you're impossible! you're not even Jewish what do you care so much?

Of course. You're right. What should I care?

No, I visited them myself.

And why?

My company manufactures parts there. They live in compounds. They come for 3 or 4 or 6 months at a time. They work 12 hour days, at least, 14 hours. They eat there in the company compound they play soccer or whatever they have social events once in a while it's all there they sleep in bunks I saw them of course they look all too much like the old German WWII forced labor camps you can't help the comparison we've seen photos of those camps. This is now. Today. In our world. Labor camps.

Forced?

By circumstance.

Economic world power struggles. International world corporate power.

It's awful. It's horrible.

It's us, pal. It's world economics. It's capitalism.

But they're a communist country.

Are you still idealistic my good friend? Still high on those early days of promise that Fidel gave the left oh those many years ago?

an i exists it doesn't belong to me even as it may be mine come on! this is not some silly language game this is life! it's alive! it's living! it's moving!

Everything's in motion. Yesterday's idealism is today's yesterday. To-morrow's fructification is today's dead fruit. Or something like that.

You can't say—something like that—because everything is its own thing nothing is like anything else. I mean was Fidel Castro an idea of 1959 or was 1959 an idea of Fidel Castro's?

No hero theories. No more heroes. No Napoleons. Great men of any kind.

Oh no? Watch the world go around.

No romantic madmen no romantic heroes!

No madmen no heroes no life no progress no moving!

What a vision you have of who we are.

i exist as essence or substance? as being or nothingness? as pure or as tainted by the stain of exisbeing? as an i alone or only as an i among all? as an i as good or as evil? what kind of an i? what kind?

There is a theory that God is that being to whom we can attribute no qualities.

is it an i alone in the cosmos or an i in a relationship with an all? i'm sorry to be so abstract. do you mind?

Yes. But when the fish arrives, let's eat the fish. look. here comes the fish!

You are saved!

that depends on what you mean by i or an i.

When I was fishing in the Mediterranean….off the island…of Procida, it was….a Procidian fisherman took me out in one of those old boats you see in the harbors all over Italy, especially in the South. Big wooden skiffs painted white and blue. As we went out I recited to him the whole of Hemingway's Old Man and the Sea, which I knew by heart. I'm a great memorizer. I memorized Dante's inferno. Dozens of Shakespearian sonnets. Do you want to hear one, anybody?

No, no. Go on with the fisherman and this island. What happened?

I told him that when we had once capsized I was swallowed by a whale.

A Mediterranean whale?

Well, okay, the fisherman kept laughing. He kept telling me it was a silly story. As was Hemingway's. Full of pretense about the sea. The sea isn't nature against you, he said. The sea is your element. It's your home. If it takes you you must be grateful. You musn't fight it. That's why, he said, every time I come home from the sea, he said, I eat and I drink and I sleep like an angel. Because i have been so at home for a time. your Hemingway doesn't know anything about the sea.

if i exist i must exist both totally and as a fragment.

Your fisherman was having you on. The romantic island peasant fisherman, in love with the sea—so at home in the vast nature of our being!

Do you like fishing?

Astronomers have just discovered that planet HD 189733B, one of planets nearest to us outside of our solar system, is blue. It is colored blue!

Do you think that astronomers are at home in the sea of outer space?

How do they know, for God's sake, what color the damn thing is!

Because, my friend, they measured the amount of light reflected off its surface.

When?

At the very moment that it eclipsed its host star.

No. When?

Last night. 4:43 a.m.

And does anybody on HD 777777—whatever know when it is 4:43 on earth? And what has that got anything to do with fishing? With nature? With water and seas? With whether I exist or not.

The sea, my friend, is blue; and the planet HD 189733B is blue; and the mystics say that the color of the earth's aura is blue.

The mystics!

I'm getting tired, honey. Shall we call it an evening?

The scientists told us that the death-mark for Earth's environment—our environment! was 600 parts per million of carbon dioxide in the atmosphere. So there's a measuring station on one of the Hawaiian islands where it's far enough away from any industrial stuff so the air is pure enough the make a reliable measuring. And so yesterday they reported from this station that we've hit 600, 600 parts per million of carbon dioxide.

So that's it? So it's over for Earth now?

He was rolling the water.

What?

He was rolling the water.

What does that mean?

Well, none of us want to believe it, of course.

It's alright. Don't worry. It's better. We'll destroy the environment and all human life will die out and then the Earth will have a million billion years to make a comeback and then human life can arise again if it does.

Are we so damned set on saving human life? What's so great about human life? Hell with it. Let it go.

Ha! I like that. It was a bold and righteous and wild experiment we were and we did some amazing and some ridiculous and some outrageous things but it ultimately failed.

Really, sweetheart, I'm really tired. Sorry.

can i say i exist if i can only exist by not saying to myself i exist? is this i which i proclaim exists. is this i a silence so vibrant it is the core if not the center of something or other? a silence so silent it can not so vibrant it can relate it can be in relation it can make others live by existing by being the creation of existence?

No, no, this is really interesting. Let's go on. Let's say that all human life was a grand experiment that failed and someday we'll be gone. Wouldn't it be a great perspective from which to write a book—a looking back a recapitulation of human life on earth a history as a form of closure or ending.

What would be the point?

For us! For the last generations of human beings to enjoy. To marvel. Hunting and gathering. Hunting! Running down a wildebeest! The harnessing of fire. The invention of agriculture. The invention of religion of ritual of society. The discovery of electricity in a universe where discovery means finding something that's been there all along. The invention of sea-going vessels from dugout canoes to the damn Titanic hell to such a thing as submarines. Airplanes. Flight! Oxygen masks. Cathedrals and horse barns. Tomatoes. Psychoanalysis. War. Poetry! Poems, damn poems, where the hell do they come from?

We know all about all that stuff.

But not from the perspective of beginning middle END man END.

What about love?

What about love?

What about the discovery of love?

Ask him. Can that be a part of your history?

If I include the history of love do I have to include the history of hate?

No, not the history. I said the discovery.

Wow. You're right. That would be fascinating.

You mean like dating?

Stop it! Don't trivialize me. I hate when you do that.

Poetry is the prophecy of the ordinary person.

Wow. Listen to that. Put that in your book. The prophecy of the ordinary person.

What about the prophecy of the ordinary animal?

We are the ordinary animal.

Does an animal have consciousness? Now that we're finally destroying the world parts per million by parts per million I'd love to answer that question before we go.

Ah, what is consciousness?

You always get so damn philosophical. Can't you just talk on an ordinary level? Talk about real things.

Like what? Like the election? Boring.

Like the trial.

America is racist. OK? Have I said enough about the trial? If you have money, you walk. If you're black, get back. What else is there to say?

There's always and ever been only one thing to say.

What's that, Mr. Philosophy?

I exist.

Or, I don't exist.

Or, I might exist.

Or, I will exist.

Nope.

Nope?

Nope. I exist. That's the only thing there is to say and I can prove it.

You can prove it's the only thing to say but can you prove the statement.

Yes. I can.

How?

Wait. You'll see.

When?

When you exist.

And if I don't….if I don't….in fact, I know I don't, I don't exist.

We're leaving. Sorry. Jeanette's tired.

Hurry up, please, it's time.

You don't have to work in the morning.

We should all go. They have to work in the morning.

We're fine.

Good-night.

Good-night. Thanks a lot. Wonderful, etc.

I felt low before I came tonight and now I feel much better. Thank you all. Good-night.

Good-night.

Good. Night.

Good, night.

Good night, good good night. Good dog, good boy, good girl, good night. Good night.

and if i don't exist? why is it why should it even be so important that i exist? what would be lost if i didn't exist? existence wouldn't be lost. we have laws of science to prove that to us. don't we? and who is this i who wouldn't exist if i didn't exist? do i even know who it is? hmm! who it was? but if it was…no, wait…am i the one who is discovered in existence? am i the one who creates existence? is it that if i didn't exist then you wouldn't exist? and/or vice versa. who would be left to witness and adjust? who would water the lawn, feed the dog, read the news and find out about the woman i knew years and years and years ago who always wanted to sing opera at la scala and here in the newspaper is a story about her about how last night she sang mimi and even though an american had never sung mimi before she so wowed the crowd that night that at her death on stage as mimi the audience was not weeping but wailing and after the performance she was carried on a litter from the Via Filodrammatici through the streets and the piazzas of florence all night long until she was deposited into the hands of the doorman of her hotel at dawn but alas to discover that in the extreme hysteria of the night she had expired. a great mourning has gripped all of milano. nothing ever like it seen before. the italian prime minister will arrive today. and to think! i knew this woman years and years and years ago. i first saw her on the new york city subway studying music sheets. we were alone in the car. sitting opposite to her, she was magnetic to me. i spoke to her. she was on her way to a small performance. i wandered the streets of greenwich village all night possessed of the image of her. i bought her flowers. i waited until the opera would let out then i went to the theater. i gave her the flowers. we lived together for two years and truly i cannot remember why we parted. and if i don't exist? what? if an i does not exist. what? what if it does. what if it is. what could it be then about subways and flowers and mimi and tragic endings to beautiful evenings?

SEVEN LIONS

With the ferociousness of seven lions, no one in the City slept that night. In the morning, everyone performed their daily rituals. One man swept out the sidewalk in front of his shop; one man in his café made coffee for each one who came in on their way to wherever; one man struggled with an anxiety attack to concentrate on the figures on the papers on his desk; the buses passed one by one, turning off at various directions, filled with passengers staring; the fortuneteller set up her equipment of cards, dice, crystal balls, séance tables; the prisoners filed into the dining hall for breakfast, under the watch of guards, not speaking; the laundress who has begun the act of cleansing with soap and water; the photographer who looks around for the right light on things; the teacher who's forgotten what she meant to do in her classroom this morning, making it up as she goes along. With the ferociousness of seven lions the day is awake. No one has a choice. Everyone has a hope for sleep. After the eyes have devoured the daylight. But no one knows. All we know is that each day dawn will come and we will rise to it and we will summon it to fill us.

www.ingramcontent.com/pod-product-compliance
Lightning Source LLC
Chambersburg PA
CBHW071216260626
47162CB00004B/1311